The Fallen O'Connell
Paperback Copyright © 2021 Lorhainne Ekelund
Editor: Talia Leduc

ISBN-13: 9781989698969

Give feedback on the book at:
lorhainneeckhart@hotmail.com

Twitter: @LEckhart
Facebook: AuthorLorhainneEckhart

Printed in the U.S.A

THE FALLEN O'CONNELL

The O'Connells

LORHAINNE ECKHART

The O'Connells of Livingston, Montana, are not your typical family. Follow them on their journey to the dark and dangerous side of love in a series of romantic thrillers you won't want to miss. Raised by a single mother after their father's mysterious disappearance eighteen years ago, the six grown siblings live in a small town with all kinds of hidden secrets, lies, and deception. Much like the contemporary family romance series focusing on the Friessens, this romantic suspense series follows the lives of the O'Connell family as each of the siblings searches for love.

The O'Connells

The Neighbor
The Third Call
The Secret Husband
The Quiet Day
The Commitment, An O'Connell Novella
The Missing Father
The Hometown Hero
Justice
The Family Secret
The Fallen O'Connell
The Return of the O'Connells
And The She Was Gone
The Stalker
The O'Connell Family Christmas
The Girl Next Door
Broken Promises

The Gatekeeper

The O'Connells Box Set Collections

About this book

Thirty-five years ago, Raymond O'Connell didn't exist, at least not until the moment Iris walked into his life. His very existence had been a secret, a carefully cultivated lie, except for the fact that he loved Iris and the six children he'd never planned on having. He'd become careless, living a life that belonged to someone else.

Becoming Raymond O'Connell had made him forget who he really was, and when he fell in love with a fantasy he knew he couldn't have, he put his family in danger. Ultimately, he found himself covering up a murder to protect the woman he loved, and that act forced him to walk away and return to the shadows of a secret life that he couldn't find his way out of.

When he returns to Livingston with a son in tow, what he doesn't expect is to be dragged from the shadows to protect a family that suddenly has a target on their backs. Soon, Raymond finds himself becoming part of a bigger, deadlier plot—one that could leave someone in his family, someone he's sworn to stay away from, dead.

The choice he'll have to make to protect the O'Connells could come at a heartbreaking cost. Can Raymond choose between the son he has now and the family he walked away from?

Chapter One

RAYMOND STARED AT THE OLD SHAG CARPET, LISTENING TO the thump of footsteps and then the water running upstairs. How had his son suddenly found his voice of damned independence for the first time in his life?

Brady was refusing to leave a home that was never supposed to have been permanent. Where had this stubborn streak come from, this sudden determination that he wouldn't have his life upended anymore? Yes, those had been his exact words, and now Raymond was at a loss for how to get his teenage son out the door and onto a plane. This was a dilemma he'd never thought he'd have.

Raymond had lived and breathed looking over his shoulder, but he couldn't explain why he found himself staring at the locked front door now, knowing the deadbolt would keep out no one who really wanted to get into the dated old house. Worse yet was the secret that lay behind why they couldn't stay in Livingston, why they had come and were now leaving. The reason, which he never planned to share with his son, was that he'd had to see in person the family he'd deserted.

Now here he was, waiting in his kitchen, knowing he was going to have to sit his son down for a talk he didn't want to have. He listened to the footsteps upstairs and glanced at his watch. It was early for Brady to be up on a Saturday morning, even though it was close to noon.

When he heard him on the stairs, his phone dinged with another email message: an inquiry from the Barbados cottage he'd booked and paid for, the one they were supposed to have arrived at the week before.

Brady gave him only a passing glance as he stepped off the last stair, barefoot, his dark hair sticking up. His eyes were his mother's, but his face and the way he walked… Raymond realized his son looked like Marcus, or maybe Luke.

He was staring at Brady's back as he reached into the fridge for a jug of milk and then into the cupboard for a bowl, and he could see how deeply ready his son was, by the expression on his face, to go another round with him. Brady set the bowl down, reached for a box of corn flakes, and dumped in the cereal, then milk. Because Raymond was standing in front of the drawer that held the spoons, he wondered whether his son would keep up the silent treatment or ask him to move.

There was the standoff.

Raymond pulled in a breath and tossed a large spoon on the counter. "Saves you having to ask, since I can see you're still doing your best to give me the silent treatment."

His son didn't flinch but snatched the spoon, then walked down over to the old table and pulled out a chair, still barefoot, in a pair of sweats and an old T-shirt.

"So, about Barbados," Raymond said, "I think we need to have another conversation, because we can't stay here."

"I'm not leaving," Brady said. "I told you that, so don't

think you can strongarm me, because you can't. I told you already that I like it here. You're the vagabond who has never been able to stay in one spot long, needing to see the world, but not me. I want roots and friends, and I'm finishing school here." He shoved another spoonful of cereal in his mouth and didn't look over to him.

Raymond had to fight the urge to yell, to demand that he get his ass upstairs and pack, because he was his father and he decided when they left and when they stayed. But he'd already done that, and it had backfired. Hence, they were still there.

What had his son said but "You can't make me"? And so far, he'd been right. Maybe he needed to try the reasoning approach.

"Okay, I see you're still angry…"

"You're kidding, right?" Brady tossed down his spoon and looked up to him. "You texted Alison that we were leaving, on my phone, as if it was from me. She's my friend! I like her, and you had no right. You crossed so many lines, Dad."

Okay, maybe he had crossed a line, but his son had never pulled something like this before, basically refusing to listen to him. Worse, Brady had no idea the danger he was putting them in.

"Fine, I get it," Raymond said. "You made your point, but you don't understand. We have to leave. This was a mistake, coming here—"

"You keep saying that." Brady cut him off, not something he had done until now. "But when I ask you why, you treat me like I'm just a little kid who's supposed to listen and fall in line without questioning anything you decide. You say it's not my concern or that, my all-time favorite, you're my father and you know best. Well, I hate to tell you this, Dad, but you don't know what's best for me. If you did, you wouldn't be trying to rip me away yet again from a place I like and a girl I'm partial to. You seem to forget I'm eighteen…"

"Not yet, you're not."

Brady slapped both his hands to the tabletop, the sound ricocheting through the half-empty house. "In three weeks I will be. I'm not a kid anymore who's going to be shuffled from one city or country to another, to places where I can't put pictures up or have a room that's always mine. Then there's Alison, who I like a lot."

All Raymond could do was stare in horror, wondering how this had spun so far out of control—out of his control. "Alison is nothing but trouble, Brady. I told you that, and her family is going through some tough times. She's not someone you can be involved with."

Brady inclined his head as if working out a kink. Raymond had never seen this kind of passion and readiness to fight in him. "I hear you, Dad, but I like Alison, and last I looked, this is a democracy, not a dictatorship. You don't get to pick my friends or who I hang out with or who my girlfriend is. And Alison isn't trouble. She makes me laugh and smile. So no, I'm not leaving." Brady picked up his spoon again and dug into his cereal.

Raymond picked up his phone, tapping the screen. "Barbados is a great place. We'd have a cottage on the white sandy beach. We've talked about going for a long time. Look, it was supposed to be a surprise, and maybe I didn't handle this right. I shouldn't have texted Alison for you. I hear you, and I'm sorry, if that will help. I promise you, this time we'll stay put for longer. You can make some friends, take up diving like we talked about."

He walked over to his son, who was working a giant mouthful of milk and cereal, and held out his cell phone to show him the image of the cottage and baby-blue ocean, but Brady only looked up to him after glancing briefly at the image as if it meant nothing.

"Not right now," he said. "I told you that. It looks nice, Dad, but I'm not going. I'm not leaving Alison right now. I've been dragged everywhere for years, but no more. I'm finishing school here. I have friends and Alison. I need to get ready." He shoved in his last mouthful of cereal before grabbing his bowl and taking it to the sink to rinse it out.

"Get ready for what?" Raymond said. They had to leave Livingston, yet his kid was far too determined, far too independent for his liking. Even though he had known this day was coming, this was a side of his son he'd never expected to see.

"I have a date for a wedding," Brady said.

"A wedding, what wedding? Who's getting married?"

Brady left the bowl in the sink and started to leave the kitchen, but he stopped in the archway and looked back at his dad before shrugging. "Alison's parents are, and I'm her date. I need to hurry, because I promised her I'd be there at one, and I still need to shower and dress."

Then his son was gone, and all Raymond could do was think of what a problem this was. His son was too stubborn, and another of his sons was getting married.

He knew there was no way this Alison and Brady thing could continue, but he also knew that leaving town without Brady ever learning the truth was now completely off the table. He couldn't stop his son from walking out the door right now and going to this wedding.

"Shit," he said. This was just another thing he'd somehow lost control of.

Chapter Two

The wind had picked up, and Iris took in the established trees in the neighborhood, swaying in the wind. The leaves had fallen, and the late September chill in the air had her shivering in her silky teal dress as she stepped inside Ryan and Jenny's house.

She heard her kids talking over soft music in the background, voices coming from the kitchen and living room. The justice of the peace was talking with Ryan and Marcus, and Luke stood off to the side. All her sons were in suits, looking dashing, handsome.

She didn't think she'd have been able to explain to anyone why it seemed they'd never get back to the normal they'd once had. But they were trying for her.

"Grandma!" Alison said. "Mom's upstairs, getting dressed, and Charlotte and Eva are up with her, but Karen and Suzanne are in the kitchen, freaking out, because the caterer apparently canceled all of a sudden."

For a minute, Iris didn't know what to say to Alison, who had run over to her, wearing a sleeveless, low-cut deep purple dress that hugged her teenage curves and stopped mid-thigh. It was sexy, revealing, something Karen would've worn, she remembered.

"But the caterer was supposed to be here already…" she started.

Ryan and Jenny's wedding was today, with just family, because it seemed the friends they'd once had were still dissecting their characters, convinced of their guilt, and had long since convicted them in the court of public opinion.

So here they were, small and quaint. She let out a sigh as she reached for her granddaughter's wrists, lifting them, taking a closer look at her makeup and forcing a smile. Alison, too, was on edge, but Iris knew that with teenagers, it could be any of a hundred problems or none of them.

"So, first, you look gorgeous, as always," she said. "I take it there's a Plan B in the works? Karen is on the phone, handling the situation?"

Alison pulled away and started walking into the kitchen without answering her, and she didn't know what that meant. When Luke glanced over, she realized something was up there, too.

She followed Alison into Ryan's kitchen, the heels of her black wedge sandals clicking on the floor. Harold was there, unloading wine and hard liquor bottles on the kitchen island. His blond hair was in the same short cop cut as always, and he wore a white dress shirt and tie. He offered a tight smile, one she tried to return. She wondered how long the tension would linger between them, considering what he'd done, arresting her. It was a memory she'd never be able to shake.

"Mom, we've got a problem," Suzanne said. Her hair was hanging long and loose over a gorgeous dress of white and black. "Jolene Harris, from the bistro, who was catering the wedding, just canceled. Actually, she didn't even have the decency to pick up the phone and call. She intended to just leave us hanging, is all we can figure. Luckily, Karen called because she wanted to remind her to pick up the cake from the bakery. That was when she broke the news, said she was sorry to do this, but she wouldn't be catering. When Karen pressed her, you know what that bitch said?" Suzanne glanced at Alison. "Ah, sorry…"

Alison only shrugged, looking impressed at her aunt's dramatics.

Iris could feel her chest tightening. Across the kitchen, Jack acknowledged her by jutting his chin, then said something to Karen, his hand around her back, rubbing. She was talking on her cell phone in that way she did when she was trying to solve something. It was just the lawyer in her, and Iris was so damn proud. Her daughter looked especially gorgeous in a sexy pink low-cut dress.

Jack started around Karen, his hand sliding over her shoulder as she said something to him, and he nodded and pressed a kiss to the side of her head. Yeah, he loved her. It was there in just a look before he started over to Iris.

"Jack, Suzanne just filled me in on the problem," Iris said. "So Jolene canceled? How can she do that? I paid her already for the catering…"

Behind her, she could hear Owen and Tessa's voices as they stepped inside. She glanced back to see her son looking dashing in a light suit, and Tessa wore a gorgeous light blue flouncy dress, her blond hair pulled up.

Iris forced herself to turn back to Jack. She never would've admitted before how much she trusted him—in a way she'd never trusted anyone, other than her children, for years now.

"She was planning to screw up Ryan and Jenny's wedding and leave you hanging, is what it sounds like," Jack said matter of factly. "But not to worry. My wife is about ready to drive over and take her down a notch, and I'm sure she's planning a number of ways to drive her out of business. Seems the public opinion in Livingston is that this family is still guilty for something, even though, logically, they know it's not true. Nonetheless, this is the situation." He held up his keys, resting his hand on her shoulder, then stepped past her. He was supportive, a good man. "Seems I'm now being recruited to go and get food. Owen! You're joining me for a trip to the supermarket. I'll explain on the way."

Iris didn't miss Owen's amused and puzzled expression, but then, he'd just walked in and wasn't up to speed like she was.

Karen hung up her cell phone. "Hey, Mom, you're here. Okay, cancel the grocery store trip, Jack. I just got off the phone with Tyrell Green, and he's on his way over. You know he owns that diner at the edge of town. I defended his son, Lawrence. He's bringing his wife with him and said they'll cook up a feast for us, a barbecue or something. I told him whatever he comes up with is fine." Karen pressed her hand to her chest and pulled in a breath as she strode over. "Mom, you look really nice, in case I didn't say it."

Jack leaned back against the island, now appearing amused, though Iris was nothing but. She remembered the Greens, how no one had wanted to defend their son. It had been a sad situation, the case her daughter had taken on. She glanced around at them, seeing that the kitchen island was already set up like a bar, courtesy of Harold.

"So it seems Jolene is screwing me," she said. "I was just saying to Jack that I paid her in full to cater this. There was no discount. I've known her for years…"

Karen waved her hand in the air. "I'll make sure she pays back every dime and then some. Don't worry. But she's no friend, Mom. Just so you know, I intend to get her blacklisted. If she wants to play these kinds of games, she's going to pay the price for messing with the O'Connells. I'm done with this crap that people think they can get away with. Even if any of the rumors about us were true, what she did is inexcusable."

Her daughter was pure fire. Iris wondered what Raymond would think if he were there. Yeah, best not to go down that road. She hadn't thought of the man in a long time, and then he'd just had to walk into her life that night, dropping by unannounced. Now not a night passed that she didn't see his image before she closed her eyes.

"You okay, Mom?" Karen said, then smiled. "Don't let Jolene stress you out. I promise I'll take her down for you and get some much-needed retribution."

Iris had to force herself to shake off Raymond. If her kids only knew what she'd been thinking… She cleared her throat. "So how's Jenny? I wonder if I should head up and talk to her."

Karen lifted her gaze toward the stairs. "I hope she has no idea that some folks are still messing with us and trying to ruin her day."

"Right, so let's make sure it stays that way," Iris said. "This is Ryan and Jenny's day, and I, for one, would prefer if no more problems came up."

She didn't know why, but everyone had hesitated as if she'd said the one thing she shouldn't have said. Then there was a timely knock at the front door, and she found herself holding her breath for a second.

Alison's face suddenly lit up, and she hurried out of the kitchen.

"I'll go up and check on Jenny, see if she needs anything," Iris said. "I take it you all have everything covered here." She gestured toward them and shrugged off her light black coat, which Owen reached for.

Her kids hesitated for only a second more, their expressions amused. Karen shook her head, and Jack was chuckling softly.

Suzanne sighed, walking over to Harold and resting her arm over his shoulder. "Yes, Mom, we've got this," she said—but then she pulled away from Harold, and her brow knit as she stared past Iris to the front door. "I didn't know Alison's friend was coming. Didn't someone say he'd left town?"

It took her a second to understand what her daughter was saying. Then she glanced back at the door, seeing Alison and a boy she'd never seen before. He was tall, lanky, cute—and holding Alison's hand. Her granddaughter was dragging him right her way with a big smile pasted to her lips, and for a minute, she could hear nothing but the loud and long thump of her heart in her ears.

"Grandma, this is Brady," Alison said, beaming. "Brady, this is my grandma."

Iris could hear her kids talking behind her. The young man had familiar features, and as he held out his hand, all Iris could do was stare at her granddaughter, who was still holding his other hand. She saw how much Alison liked him, and in that moment, she realized that Raymond O'Connell, or whoever he really was, had just lied to her again.

Chapter Three

Iris's phone was buzzing, and she took in the caller ID, a private number. She considered it for only a second before answering as she pulled open the back door.

In the kitchen, Ryan was all smiles, a groom ready to marry his bride. Jenny was still upstairs, but the moment for her to come down was likely anytime. Iris had finally had to force herself away from Brady and Alison, realizing her granddaughter was head over heels for a young man it was impossible for her to have those feelings for.

"Hello?" was all she got out.

"Iris, it's Raymond. I understand Ryan is getting married today, and I have to warn you that—"

"Brady's here," she said, cutting him off, feeling the bite in her words as she pulled the door closed behind her. "I presume that's why you're calling. Why are you still here? You told me you were leaving. This is my son's wedding day. Do you have any idea what you've done, what you're doing to those kids, my granddaughter…?"

Then she spotted him. He was walking up the side of the house just as she stepped around the corner. He looked way too good for a man she was furious with. He pulled his cell phone away from his ear and hung up.

She strode toward him, glancing at the side window of the dining room and hoping no one was looking out. "You can't be here," she whispered loudly. "Why are you here?"

He let his gaze linger for a moment on her before he reached for her arm and had her walking back into the yard, out of sight. She didn't miss the way he glanced back over his shoulder, still holding her. She yanked her bare arm away, lifting her hands and brushing back strands of her dark hair from her forehead. It had been freshly cut at a salon in Bozeman, not a far drive, but at least no one had known who she was.

"I'm here because Brady refuses to listen," he said. "I tried to leave, but he wouldn't hear of it. He actually put his foot down because he wants roots all of a sudden."

She just stared at him as if he'd lost his mind. "You had no trouble walking away from me and my children."

"Our children," he said.

She found herself pulling back further, not sure what to make of his expression. She thought she hissed, and she had to fist her hands. "You may have fathered them, but that's all you did, Raymond. You left. Remember, you have a new life, a son with someone else—a son who's here right now. Do you know my granddaughter has romantic notions about your son? I've never seen her so head over heels, and let me be really clear: This isn't a childhood crush. Right now, they're in there holding hands, and she's probably looking for a way to sneak off with him to make out and do the kinds of things they can't be doing, considering they're related. Him being in there only confirms what I already suspected. Brady has no idea, because you didn't tell him. Now, how do you think he's going to react when he finds out? Alison is going to be devastated. You really have messed this up, Raymond, but then, isn't that what you do?"

She'd expected something from him: anger, annoyance. She was holding nothing back, but there was no way she was using kid gloves now, considering her granddaughter was involved.

Raymond glanced into the distance and said nothing, then lifted his gaze over her head to the house. This man she'd thought she'd known well at one time was in fact a stranger she knew nothing about. Maybe that was why she felt the need to pull her arms over her chest. She shivered, welcoming the chill, then heard a car door in front and voices. It had to be Tyrell Green and his wife, who were saving their asses.

"You need to take him home now," Iris started, but then, behind her, she heard the door slap closed.

"Hey, Mom, the Greens are here. I could…"

Iris turned to see Karen stepping out of the house. Her expression was amused as she made her way over.

"There you are," Karen said. "I didn't know you were out here talking with…"

She could feel the way Raymond gave everything to her, and her daughter suddenly hesitated. Maybe she had now realized or had some idea.

"Hello," was all she said, and Iris couldn't pull her gaze from her, seeing the way her brow knit as she took in the two of them as if trying to figure out a puzzle. Iris couldn't get her tongue to move. She couldn't get one word out of her mouth, which had suddenly gone so dry.

"You look gorgeous, Karen," Raymond said. Now, why did he have to say that?

"I'm sorry, have we met?" Karen said.

Iris lifted her gaze to Raymond, wishing so many

things, one of which was for him to leave before he could ruin Jenny and Ryan's day.

"Mom, say something," Karen said. "Who is this?"

Iris had to breathe, very aware that Raymond hadn't pulled his gaze from Karen. She could see he wasn't going to make this easy. "Someone who shouldn't be here," she finally said. "I'm sorry, Karen, but this is—"

"Dad..." Karen said. From the way she breathed his name out, Iris could feel her emotion, her heartache. She pressed her hand over her heart and didn't pull her gaze from Raymond.

"Hi there, darlin'," he said. Of course, she remembered what he'd called her, and she could feel her nails digging into her palms over the fondness in his voice.

"Look, he was just leaving," she said quite abruptly. "He just needs to fix a situation here."

Karen shook her head and then seemed to gather herself as she looked between her parents. "I thought you left," she said. "I heard you were here. Luke and Marcus saw you. I just have so many questions to ask you, why you left, why you came back, why you're here now..." She dragged her gaze over to Iris. "Did you know he was still here?" she said, sounding so accusatory.

"No, your mother didn't know I was here," Raymond said. "I just showed up because my son is here."

Of course, Karen was confused. Iris could see it in her expression as she dragged her gaze back and forth between them. "Well, of course, all your sons are inside, and one of them is getting married today. Did you know about the wedding? Is that why you're here?"

Raymond glanced over her head to the back door, and she hoped no one else would come out. "Only just found out, which is why I'm here—but I'm talking about my other son, who's here right now but shouldn't be."

"Brady is who he's talking about, Karen," Iris finally said, cutting in, mainly because Karen was looking at this man as if considering inviting him in.

Karen glanced over to her so quickly. The shock, the horror, the alarm… Yeah, she could see the moment she got it. "Brady…Alison's Brady, inside, is your son?" Her expression seemed completely rocked, her voice filled with the kind of passion only she had.

"Yes, afraid so," Iris said. "Seems Brady is Raymond's son, so you can see the problem, considering that makes him your half-brother, and neither he nor Alison has any idea."

Karen hissed and pressed her hand over her chest again. "No…!" She whispered loudly, then pulled in another breath. "No, that's not fair."

"My thoughts exactly," Iris said. "So now we need to get Brady out of that house and away from Alison. Raymond is having trouble leaving, as it seems his son also has feelings for Alison and is refusing to move. Raymond has never told him anything about us, or we wouldn't be in the situation we are now."

When Iris dragged her gaze back to Raymond, she could see he had a few things he likely wanted to say to her, by the way he stared at her long and hard. But then, she had no idea where exactly she and her children ranked against his other family, Brady.

"You seriously think he can just walk in and ask Brady to leave without everyone wondering why?" Karen said. "Then there's Alison. There's no way she'll take that lying down. This just isn't okay, another problem… How the hell are we going to fix this? Ryan and Jenny are getting married. This is their day and Alison's. No, no, no…we're not ruining this for them." She lifted her hands and tapped her fingers to her forehead, just something she did when getting ready to really dig in her heels.

"No, I agree," Iris said. "This is my son's wedding day, and I will not have Alison upset right now."

"I agree it's not the right time," Raymond replied, crossing his arms over his jacket. His dark jeans fit better than they should, she thought.

"So then you'll leave, and we'll make sure the kids don't get a moment alone, and then…"

"No, I'll stay," Raymond said, cutting her off.

Karen was as thrown as she was, she thought, but Raymond kept glancing around. What the hell was he looking for? She found herself looking over her shoulder and then back to him.

"That's impossible," she said. "You can't stay."

Then the door squeaked open again, and this time she turned to see Alison in the doorway, looking out. "Grandma, the wedding's going to start," she called, then stopped and took in Raymond. "Oh, hey there, Ray. Didn't know you were coming to my parents' wedding. Brady didn't say anything."

Iris thought she made a strangled noise.

"Hi, Alison, great to see you," Raymond said. He forced a smile that seemed far too relaxed, then gave everything to Iris. "Your grandma was just mentioning the wedding. Didn't mean to intrude. I just had something important to discuss with Brady."

"Oh, but the wedding is going to start," Alison said. "You can stay. I'm sure my mom and dad would like to meet you. Grandma, Aunt Karen, Dad said to tell you to come in, because Mom's ready to come down the stairs. Everyone else is in the living room."

"Right," Karen whispered to her and wrapped her hand around Iris's arm.

"Okay, we'll be right there," Iris called.

As her granddaughter went back inside, Raymond dragged his hand over his face.

"You need to go," she said quite forcefully, but all he did was shake his head.

"Unfortunately, I think it's a little late for that," he replied, then turned to Karen, who she knew was on the fence with all of this.

"Dad?" The door squeaked again. "What are you doing here?"

Okay, this really wasn't the time. Iris could feel this spiraling into something way out of her control. Raymond lifted his gaze to Brady, who looked dashing. Seeing the two of them together, she could see the resemblance, and the resemblance to Luke, Marcus, Ryan, and Owen. How much longer before everyone else figured it out, too?

"I told your dad to stay for the wedding," Alison said, appearing behind him. "Come on, Grandma…"

She felt Karen touch her arm, could feel the ground not quite as solid as it had been before. She glanced in horror at her daughter, who just patted her arm as she stood beside her.

"Maybe this won't be as bad as you think," Karen whispered, forcing a smile for Alison, who was still standing in the doorway with Brady. From the expression on her face, Iris knew her granddaughter was expecting some kind of disaster.

"Okay, let's go in. Save me a seat," she said to Alison as she headed up and reached for the open door, and Brady and Alison started into the house. She turned, taking in the horror that had crept back into Karen's expression. Raymond was standing at the bottom of the porch steps. "Let me be very clear: You will not ruin my son's wedding day. So help me… As soon as Ryan and Jenny are married,

I want you out of here with Brady. Do I make myself clear?"

Karen said nothing as she stood between them, and Raymond's eyes, the color she had always thought of as O'Connell blue, flickered with something she hadn't seen in a long time.

As Karen slipped past her inside, she could hear voices, music. Raymond lifted his hand and reached for the door, holding it, angling his head and really looking long and hard at her. He was a man who didn't cower under anyone.

"I hear you, Iris, but let me be very clear, as well: I'm not leaving here without Brady. I'm not here to ruin my son's wedding, but if we keep standing out here, discussing this, who else do you think is going to come outside?"

She stepped in, feeling Raymond right behind her.

In the kitchen, the Greens were already cooking. She took in Tyrell, whose short dark hair was tinged with more white than she remembered. His wife was curvy, her dark hair pulled back, and she tossed an easy smile Iris's way, with dimples in her plump dark cheeks, just as she put a large tin roaster covered with foil in the oven.

Iris dreaded what else was going to happen, so she turned to Raymond and said, "Help Tyrell in the kitchen. Stay out of sight. As soon as they're married, I'll send Brady in, and you figure out a way to get him out of here. Then you'll both leave." She kept her voice low and stood right in front of him, having to look way up.

All he did was look past her and jut his chin toward the living room. "You'd better go," he said.

When she turned to see who he was looking at, she realized it was Marcus, standing there with Karen, and the expression on his face, the way he looked past her, straight at Raymond, was anything but friendly.

Chapter Four

"Just so you know, we like these folks," said Tyrell Green's wife, Michelle, as she stepped over to Raymond, who had offered to help by shucking corn from, evidently, a late fall harvest. "Karen is a saint. If it hadn't been for her, our son would be in a supermax in another state, and we'd never get to see him. He'd be doing more time than he is."

There was just something about the way she said it, the way she looked at him. He realized she was giving him a warning, even though he knew she had no idea who he was.

"So Karen was your son's lawyer?" he said, though he suspected there was more to the story.

He could hear the wedding in the next room, and he didn't think he'd ever forget the way Marcus and Karen had stood in that hallway, staring him down as they waited for Iris to walk into the living room. It was as if they thought he was there to ruin something, which was the one thing he wasn't about to do.

There was just something about being here, knowing

all his kids were under this roof at the same time. He could feel everything he'd firmly held in his control slipping, and that was something he never allowed to happen.

"Karen took on his case when no one else would," Michelle said. "She didn't take much, either, though we gave her all we could. She's still fighting for him, too. When she called because Jolene Harris screwed them over after promising to cater this, we closed up the diner and came, because that's what you do for people you care about."

By the way she said it, he figured she wasn't done making her point, but he took some comfort in knowing that there were people in this town who had his kids' backs. "What, you mean another caterer was supposed to be here and canceled?"

Tyrell cleared his throat, pouring marinade over potatoes that had been cut up in a roasting pan, then covered it with tinfoil. "Michelle, it don't matter what happened, so let's not talk badly about folks," he said.

Michelle's expression turned heated, and she rested her hands on her hips, giving him everything. "It does matter! The folks here treated this family horrible, and you even said that we should reach out and see if we could do something for them. When Karen called, we dropped everything to come. You and I both know that Jolene Harris is a loud, mouthy bitch who has trash-talked this family. She should be ashamed of what she did. Yes, she was supposed to be here, catering Ryan's wedding. Iris paid her, from what Karen said, and it sounds like she had no intention of even showing up. I've seen a lot of nastiness from people, growing up. Some people do it because they think someone's done something to deserve it, but we know, from going through what we did with Lawrence, seeing people we knew turn on us... We understand how friends disappear and suddenly see you as guilty even though you didn't do anything."

Raymond sensed this woman could go on and on, and he continued to shuck the corn in the sink.

"Michelle, put the potatoes in the oven and check the ribs," Tyrell said, interrupting. "We need to get the slaw done, and those meatballs, did you get them on yet?"

"Oh, I put them on in the slow cooker…" She started across the kitchen to the table, where the slow cooker was plugged in along with another heated serving dish, alongside some bottles of liquor.

"Don't pay Michelle no mind," Tyrell said. "She's just in the O'Connells' corner. You know, when Lawrence went away, it was Iris who showed up on our doorstep with a casserole. Didn't expect it, but she just wanted us to know there were people in our corner, too. We never forgot that. He was arrested over in Bozeman. Even Marcus tried to step in for him. Lawrence was in the wrong place at the wrong time, you know. Not that this is any of my business, but I seen the way Marcus looked at you, not too friendly. So thank you for helping, but if you're thinking of causing any problems here, don't."

Okay, he'd been duly warned.

He could hear laughter and cheering and knew that his son was now married. Though he'd stayed out of sight and out of the way, he wished he could've watched. He wiped his hands and took in his jacket, which was resting over the back of the chair, then glanced back over to Tyrell, who was a few inches shorter than him, staring at him with those dark eyes, as if he knew his secrets.

"Sounds like they're married now," Raymond said, stepping away from the sink. "In case I didn't say it, thank you for showing up. I think now would be a good time for me to grab my son and slip out."

Tyrell nodded, then stepped in to finishing shucking the rest of the corn.

Raymond reached for his coat, but just then, he spotted Owen and a gorgeous blonde, whom he knew had to be Tessa, coming his way. Owen said something to her, and she hung back as Owen strode right over to him. The way his firstborn looked at him was anything but friendly.

"Just what the hell are you doing here?" Owen said. "I can't believe you had the nerve to show up." His voice was low, and he pulled his hand over the back of his dark hair, which had the same slight wave it had always had. He was tall, just like Raymond. All his boys were. He spotted Brady with Alison, lingering, laughing, talking, and there was Iris, watching them closely.

"Didn't have a choice," Raymond said. "Did you talk to your mother?"

Owen glanced over his shoulder, and he spotted Marcus coming their way, and Luke too. Everyone was dressed to the nines. Great, it seemed he was about to be cornered, and the possibility of slipping out quietly was slipping away.

"What is this about?" Owen said. "Why don't you just tell me what's going on? So Mom knows you're here and she just let you stay?"

Marcus and Luke were right there now, and Raymond just nodded to them, never expecting this kind of hate to be staring back at him from his kids. He wished it could be so different.

"Why are you still here?" Marcus said. "You were leaving town, remember?"

Luke said nothing, just studying him as if he were a puzzle he needed to figure out.

"I'm here for my son, who insisted on coming,"

Raymond said. "The plan was to leave, but Brady wouldn't agree."

Ryan was there in the background, and Jenny, his bride in a white dress, and Alison, who seemed over the moon. He knew the minute Ryan saw him.

"Brady is your son?" Luke said in a low voice. "Right, of course he is. Wow, you really screwed the pooch big time on this one, Pops. He's here with our Alison, so you're going to destroy two more kids' lives."

Ryan stepped over. The expression on his face was murderous, and could he blame him? No.

"Congratulations, Ryan," he forced himself to say.

He expected his son to yell at him to get out, but Ryan only nodded.

In the living room, Brady was lingering, and Raymond knew he was starting to pick up on something. He didn't remember ever seeing him appear so confused, but he didn't have a clue how to get him out of this house without telling him the truth, because he had to be wondering now. Raymond would be left with no choice but to tell him why nothing could ever happen between him and Alison, and then Brady would be angry—no, furious.

"This is my wedding day," Ryan said. "I can't believe you'd show up here. Why? No, don't say it. I know why. Brady is your son, right? You didn't even think of what this would do."

Raymond pulled in a breath and crossed his arms over his chest. "I need to have a word with Brady, Ryan, and then we'll be out of here. Again, I'm sorry. You have no idea how sorry I am."

It was Luke who stepped back and walked over to Brady. Whatever he said to him had him walking over, and the expression on his face was one Raymond had never seen before.

"Dad, what the hell are you doing here?" Brady said. "Mr. O'Connell, I'm so sorry for this…"

Ryan only rested his hand on Brady's shoulder and said, "Don't worry about it, Brady. You need to go talk to your dad." Then he patted his shoulder again and stepped away.

Raymond gestured to the back door, then pulled it open, because this conversation was one he wasn't going to have in front of everyone.

Brady glanced back and called out, "Alison, I'll be right back."

Raymond looked over to a family he was trying to figure out how to make things right with, and he saw a girl who was about to be devastated because of this secret he'd kept. His granddaughter. He fought the urge to say he was sorry.

As they stepped out, Tyrell looked over to him, and for just that one moment, Raymond swore the man knew exactly who he was and what he was about to do. He forced himself to pull the door closed behind them.

Brady turned on him. "Seriously, Dad, this is too much. You can't just show up here like this. This is Alison's parents' wedding. You're interfering with their day and mine. Is this because I've stood my ground and won't leave? Like, are you seriously trying to ruin my life?"

He lifted his hand to calm his son, who had every right to be angry and was going to be a whole lot more. "No, the last thing I want to do is ruin your life," he said. "It's quite the opposite. I'm here so you won't ruin your life and do something stupid because of something I should have told you."

Brady dragged both his hands over his head in the way he did when he was frustrated. Raymond remembered it was something Owen had done, too, when he was young. Why he thought of that now, he didn't know.

"This is about Alison again?" Brady said. "I cannot believe you, Dad. You have no say in who I date or see, and you don't get an opinion on Alison—"

"She's my granddaughter," Raymond said, cutting him off. He couldn't figure out how to explain this, so he went right to ripping the bandage off. There was no way to tell him nicely.

"Excuse me?" Brady said, and Raymond wasn't sure whether his expression was shock or if he actually hadn't heard him.

"Eighteen years ago, I had another family," Raymond said. "I walked away from them, and I never told you about them. I had a wife and six kids, whom you've just met. I never planned on telling you, and I wish now I had, because the last thing I ever wanted was to see the hurt I can see now in you. That's why I pushed. That's why I wanted to leave. It's not because I didn't like Alison; it's because she's family. Ryan, Marcus, Luke, and Owen are your brothers, and Karen and Suzanne are your sisters."

Brady just stood there.

"I'm so sorry," Raymond finally said. "Say something."

Brady opened his mouth to reply, but nothing came out. He dropped his gaze to the ground, and it seemed as if time stood still. When he slowly lifted his gaze back up to him, staring at him, it was with an expression he'd never expected to see on his son's face. Instead of saying anything, Brady started to walk away. Raymond reached for his arm only to have Brady snatch it away as if he were going to hit him.

"Brady!" he called out.

"No! Stay the fuck away from me. Are you kidding?

How could you do this to me? Just stay away from me, because right now, I hate you."

Instead of going back into the house, Brady started running around front to the sidewalk, and then he was gone up the street. Raymond figured he'd find him locked in his room at home.

When he looked to the back door, feeling like the worst person ever, he spotted Ryan stepping out of the house and walking his way.

"I'm so sorry, Ryan, for bringing this here, for ruining this day for you," he said.

"Stop," Ryan said, sounding so calm, though there was an edge to his voice. "You ruined our lives years ago. But this… Just go, please."

Instead of saying anything else or apologizing to a son who would likely never forgive him, Raymond only nodded. The O'Connells would never be part of his life again.

He shoved his hands in his pockets and started walking, and this time, he didn't look back.

Chapter Five

It had been a really long day. Alison had cried her eyes out, and the wedding had been somewhat subdued after Raymond and Brady's hasty departure. The food Tyrell and Michelle had cooked up had been amazing, though Iris had spent what should have been an enjoyable feast picking at her food and sitting with her granddaughter, who was nursing a broken heart.

She stood with her, her arm around her shoulders, after Ryan told her who Raymond and Brady really were. She'd been unable to answer the one question Alison had asked her while everyone was eating: Why was Raymond there now with Brady, anyway, if he'd walked away all those years ago? Why had he come back?

The fact was that he lived not even a block away and had been there for months. Even Iris had to wonder what that was about. Despite everything she didn't know about Raymond, she did know when something was up.

It seemed her granddaughter knew more than she did, yet all Iris could do as she sat with her and swallowed her own misery was tell her she had no idea what went on in the mind of Raymond O'Connell or why he did the things he did.

Her heart went out to Brady, too, who hadn't chosen any of this. She couldn't help wondering who his mother was, the other woman—and there it was, another moment of fury and jealousy she'd never expected to feel.

"Well, that was just a shit-kicker of a day, wasn't it?" Luke said as he came into the kitchen, where she'd just filled the kettle and plugged it in. It was nearly midnight, and it was pitch black outside. She should get some sleep, but she was too unsettled and needed some time to quiet her thoughts before bed.

She lifted her hand, taking in Luke as he pulled at his tie. Her heels had been dumped at the door, so she wore just her stockings on the cold floor. She wasn't sure what it was about him that was different. Maybe she expected him to be as angry as Marcus and Ryan or even Owen, who hadn't wanted to have a conversation about his dad. Suzanne and Karen, too, had been in a constant huddle, likely talking about Raymond in ways she would rather not know.

"I would say I'm sorry, but I had no idea he was still in town," Iris said. "He told me very clearly that he was leaving."

Luke leaned against the island, his brow furrowed. He wasn't smiling. "You talked to him and saw him before today?"

She inhaled. Right, she hadn't told her kids about that night he'd shown up in the backyard in the dark while she was home alone. "Once," she said. "He showed up the night after the charges were dropped, when you were at Ryan's. I'm not sure why he came by, maybe to say good-bye, to say he was sorry. I have no idea, Luke, but he told me then about Brady. I was so furious at what he'd done.

So yes, I knew, but I never expected this to happen. He was supposed to leave. When I saw Brady today at Ryan's, and I saw that Alison had invited him as her date, I swear I wanted to kill your father for a moment. I knew Brady didn't know. Today was unavoidable, but it seems that with Raymond, there's a trail of repercussions, of lives destroyed. At least it's out in the open now, and maybe he'll leave us, and we can get back to…" She paused. Back to what? "I suppose whatever our new normal is," she finished, then gestured as the kettle whistled. She pulled the plug.

Just then, there was a knock at the door.

"You expecting someone?" she said to Luke, who instantly went on alert, pushing his hand out to her.

"Stay here," he said and walked into the living room.

She realized he had a gun in his hand. Geez, had he been carrying it all day? He flicked on the outside light and then let out a breath, and she didn't miss the way he relaxed. She strode into the living room carefully, her hand on her chest.

"It's Brady," he tossed out over his shoulder after tucking his gun in the waistband of the back of his dress pants. As he pulled open the door, she took in the young man standing there, still in his dress pants and nice shirt, with no coat. He looked cold and miserable.

"I'm sorry to just show up here," Brady said.

"Nonsense. Come on in," Luke replied.

Iris took in the tall gangly boy, whom she could see Luke was trying to make sense of. "You have no coat?" she said. "It's freezing out there. Where's your dad?"

Brady stood so awkwardly in the entryway, and she thought for a moment that he was too embarrassed to look at her. "I didn't know where to go. I remembered Alison showing me that her grandma lived here. I thought it would be okay if I stopped by?" His hands were in his pockets, and she thought he was shivering. As he stepped down into the living room, she could see by his face that he'd been crying. Maybe he was waiting for her to tell him to leave.

"You know what, Brady? Come on in," she said. "You look cold. Luke, can you grab a sweater for Brady?"

Luke pulled a hoodie from the closet and strode down and handed it to him. Brady shrugged it on.

Iris lifted her gaze to her son, unsure of what to do. "Come on, Brady, sit down. Does your dad know where you are?" She rested her hand over his shoulder, rubbing it.

He sat on the sofa, hunched over, and shook his head. He put his hand over his face for a second and then pulled it away. There was such misery there, and she took in his eyes, not the same O'Connell blue as her children's.

"No, I don't want to talk to him," he said. "I'm so angry at him. How could he have lied to me? I really liked Alison, and now I don't know what to feel. I didn't know he had a family before me. He just told me today that he walked away from you all eighteen years ago. Did he do it because of me? I never knew any of this. I'm almost eighteen. That's all I can think of…"

Okay, this wasn't good. She sat down on the sofa beside him and reached over, then gently squeezed his arm. It was the only thing she could think of doing. "Look, this is kind of a mess, this situation, but this isn't your fault. At the same time, you have to call your dad and tell him you're here. He has to be worried."

"My mom's right," Luke said. "Look, kid, it's a shitty situation, but how about you give me your dad's number, and I'll call him and tell him you're here, and then everyone can stop worrying?"

From the way Brady looked up to Luke, she didn't

think he'd tell him. "So you're my brother," was all he said. Iris looked over to Luke and wasn't sure if there was amusement behind the way he winced.

"It seems I am, kid," Luke said. She knew he was waiting as he pulled out his cell phone.

Brady dragged his gaze over to her. "And you were married to my dad?"

Wow, that was a question she didn't know how to answer, considering she gathered Brady knew nothing about his dad's exploits or who he really was. She suspected Raymond had kept many other secrets.

"Yes, and he left one night, walked out on us," she said, and the boy just nodded. "But that's between your dad and me. It has nothing to do with you."

Brady shrugged and then gestured toward her. "How can you say that? You should be angry with me. You have every right to be angry with me. So, my mom, did you know her?"

The way he said it had her shaking her head and then looking up to Luke, who was watching the boy in a way that seemed conflicted.

"I'm sorry, but I didn't," Iris said. "In fact, I didn't know about you. This has been a big surprise for all of us."

"Come on, kid," Luke said. "What's Raymond's number? No matter how angry you are at him, I need to call him and tell him you're all right."

She found herself looking from Luke to Brady, trying to pick out the similarities. The way he was sitting, she thought, was like Marcus. There was so much of her kids that she could see in him. Brady just lifted his gaze to Luke with that pure stubbornness she was familiar with.

"Brady, come on," she said. "Luke is right. It doesn't matter how angry you are with your dad. There's nothing worse than not knowing where your kid is. I would know; I raised six, with all the problems that go with them, all the attitudes and arguments and taking off and worries. This doesn't mean he doesn't care. We all make mistakes, but he's still your dad, and—"

"And, what, I have to forgive him?" he snapped, cutting her off.

Luke stepped forward. "Hey, enough, Brady," he said, gesturing toward him so sharply and matter of factly. "I get that you're angry, and you have every right, but maybe one day you will forgive him. You need to remember something. Whatever happened, let me ask you this: Has there ever been a time that your dad hasn't been there for you?"

She wasn't sure Brady was ready to listen or that he was going to answer. He looked down at his lap, and for a minute, she thought he was slipping into that mute, stubborn, silent teenage mood. What the hell was she supposed to do?

"Brady, come on," she said. "Give your dad's number to Luke so he can tell him you're okay. You have to be hungry. I'll make you a sandwich, and we'll talk."

And then Raymond could pick him up, take him home, and straighten out this mess.

This time, when Brady looked over to her, she saw the same O'Connell stubbornness that Luke and Suzanne had, the way his mouth went tight. He stared up at Luke. "All right, you can tell him I'm okay, but that's all."

Iris hadn't realized she'd been holding her breath, and as she let it go, it sounded too much like relief.

Then Brady pulled his gaze from Luke, giving everything to her, and said, "But you can also tell him I'm not coming home."

Chapter Six

"Dammit, Brady, where are you? This is not funny. Call me right now!" Raymond snapped.

He'd lost count of the number of times he'd called his son, and every one had gone right to voicemail. This was the kind of panic he'd never expected to feel, even though it had always been there in the back of his mind. He paced his darkened house without a clue where to look.

After Brady ran out of Ryan's, Raymond had been furious and terrified. His son had no clue of the dangers that lurked in wait for him all because of who his father was. He willed the front door to open. After the relief would come the moment when he could yell at his son for the worry he'd caused and for being reckless and stupid. He wanted to wrap his arms around his son and shake him.

Brady had looked at him with the kind of hate he'd never expected to see, just like Marcus, Luke, Ryan, Suzanne, Karen, and Owen. Seeing them all again, the way they'd looked at him, and knowing he was at the center of an event that had likely ruined Ryan's wedding day, he'd been faced with all the choices he'd made.

He dragged his hand over his face, very aware that time was ticking in the silence. What would this mean for everyone he cared for? Him being there now instead of disappearing with Brady could mean the difference between life and death, and that was the kind of risk he couldn't take.

As he stepped over to the living room window and brushed back the curtains, looking out at the quiet street, he couldn't shake the fear that had saved him time and again, keeping him on edge and wide awake so he wouldn't make the kind of mistake that would cost someone he loved his or her life. At the same time, he knew he was out of choices now.

He held his cell phone and scrolled through his numbers, seeing Marcus's name. He had all his kids' names, numbers, addresses. He knew everything about them.

He listened to the ring: once, twice…

"Yeah, who is this?" Marcus sounded as if he'd been asleep. Raymond heard a murmur in the background.

"I'm sorry to call. This is…Raymond, your father."

There was silence. Of course, he'd be the last person Marcus expected to call him.

"Look I wouldn't be calling you, except I can't find Brady. He hasn't come home. Have you seen him? Did he go back to Ryan's? He left, and I expected him to be at home, but he wasn't. I've waited. He's not answering his phone, and I'm starting to fear the worst…"

"No, I haven't seen him," Marcus said. Raymond heard him say something, maybe to his pregnant wife, Charlotte. Then it sounded as if a door closed, and he sighed on the other end. Raymond pictured his son's house, knowing how vulnerable they would be. "You're actually calling me? Look, he didn't come back to the house. Your timing… I still can't believe what happened, with you putting a damper on Ryan and Jenny's day. Then there's Alison—but you didn't call to talk about that. How did you get my number, anyway?"

What was he supposed to say? He looked out the window, seeing nothing but shadows, though he knew all too well that nothing good ever hid there. "I have all your numbers. It's what I do. I also know where you live and what you all do. I know it wasn't Osbert Berry who made that charge go away when you lifted a case of spray paint when you were seventeen, and I know your graffiti antics went beyond the high school and abandoned buildings. In four of the five burglaries in the area, the security cameras were spray-painted over. Should we talk about how I know it was you?"

There was silence on the other end, and he wondered whether Marcus would hang up. "Brady didn't come back to Ryan's," he finally said. "I haven't seen him. You know a missing person's report can't be filed yet, officially."

Okay, so he didn't want to talk about what a little shit he used to be.

"You think I want to file a missing person's report, and that's why I called you?"

In the background, he heard a door closing, then creaking, as if Marcus was walking downstairs. "Isn't it? Why'd you call, then?"

Raymond had expected anger, but Marcus sounded on edge. "A little help finding Brady," he replied. "Put aside your feelings for me…"

"Fine, what about his friends? Have you tried them? He probably wanted some space, is all, considering the bomb you dropped. I can only imagine what he's thinking.

It's something Luke used to do, take off for days some-times, but he always turned up."

What was he supposed to say to that? Although there was so much he knew about his kids, there was a lot he didn't. Either way, Brady wasn't Luke. "We're still here," Raymond said. "We didn't leave because of Alison, because Brady has a thing for her. She's who he hangs around with, other than Craig Lister, that jock from school, a time or two. He wouldn't be there."

"Well, how do you know that? Give me his number, and call—"

"You think I'd be calling you if I thought Brady was there? I've already been over to Craig's house and stood out in the shadows, only to see that no one was there. Craig and his family are away on a weekend trip to a cottage they own in Idaho."

He'd leave out the part about how he'd slipped into their house and gone through their things. The cottage was in Sun Valley, and the dad had paid cash to a banker who knew how to hide his money well. Then there was the marijuana he'd found, which, apparently, Craig's mom had a thing for.

"Do I want to know how you know that?" Marcus said.

Raymond just shook his head even though he knew Marcus couldn't see him, and he said nothing more on that. "Look, as I said, the only reason we're still here is because of Brady's feelings for Alison, because he suddenly wanted to put down roots. There's no one else. The only thing I can think is that he's wandering around or in trouble. I've walked the neighborhood, tracing every step I know he would take. I hoped maybe he'd gone back to Ryan's. Evidently, he doesn't want to be found, and what I can't believe is that he's suddenly good at hiding."

Marcus sighed on the other end. "Tell me where you are. I'll come over."

He hesitated only a second before giving Marcus his address. He expected him to say something about where he lived, the proximity to Iris, but all Marcus said was "I'm on my way." Then he hung up.

Raymond just stared out the window into the darkness again, the streetlights, the shadows, the houses across the street, the parked cars. When someone showed up, who would it be? Whoever it was wouldn't come through the front door.

The old clock on the wall ticked, and the fridge clicked on and off. Then his phone dinged, and when he pulled it out, he saw a message from Luke: *Brady's here at Mom's. You have a problem, though, because he said he's not going home.*

He squeezed the phone as he spotted the headlights of the sheriff's cruiser, and he stepped out of the house, locking the door behind him. Raymond approached the car, and Marcus stepped out, wearing his sheriff's jacket, a pair of jeans, and a ball cap.

"What's going on?" Marcus said.

Raymond pulled open the passenger door. "We're going to your mom's," he said.

Marcus shook his head, giving him an odd smile that wasn't a smile. "No, we're not."

"We are, because I found Brady. Luke just texted. He's over at your mom's and says he's not leaving."

Marcus groaned and pulled open his door, taking in Raymond across the roof of the cruiser. "This just keeps getting better and better," he finally said, tapping the car and then gesturing to him. "Fine, but hear me on this: You're not messing with Mom. We go and get Brady, and then you're leaving town. Are we clear?"

He could feel the bite in his words, and he glanced

away for a second, saying nothing, before taking in the son whose life he hadn't been a part of for the past eighteen years.

"So should I ask how you knew about the paint?" Marcus said, and Raymond could see that he was thrown. "Even Bert didn't know about the spray-painted cameras."

He wondered whether Marcus had any idea of the road he had been on, of how close he had come to finding himself labeled a career criminal, behind bars. He wondered, too, whether Bert, the old sheriff, had known who the request came from to recruit Marcus to the sheriff's office and keep a close eye on him. Now, after having been on the wrong side of it, his son was the law.

"So how did you make the charges go away? How…?" Marcus started, then lifted his hands again. "You know what? I don't want to know."

Before Marcus could slip behind the wheel, Raymond said, "I've been watching all of you for years. I may have been unable to be here, but that doesn't mean I didn't do what I could from afar. You likely think you have an idea of who I am, but I guarantee you have no idea at all."

Then he climbed in the passenger side of the cop car, taking in the equipment, the radio, and the assault rifle within easy reach. Instead of saying anything else, Marcus merely started the vehicle and pulled away.

All Raymond could think was that he'd no longer just slipped into town and stayed under the radar. Now he was front and center, making the kind of noise that would have eyes on him—and, worse, on everyone he cared about.

Chapter Seven

Iris spread mayonnaise on wholegrain bread, then added a slice of cheese and leftover sliced ham from the fridge, as well as some lettuce. She was very aware of how quiet Brady was as he sat on the stool at the island, just staring at the sandwich fixings on the cutting board. She added some mustard, then another slice of bread, then sliced it in half.

Brady was so different from her children. She didn't know how to make sense of the fact that this was Raymond's son. All she could think about was that he'd been with another woman. She'd been punishing herself because of everything that happened, only to learn that he had left her for Brady's mother. She rested the sandwich on the plate and slid it in front of him.

"Here, eat something," she said. "How about something to drink—water, juice, or I think there's some soda? Not ideal this late, but…"

He lifted a sandwich half and took a bite, still wearing Luke's hoodie, which was way too big for him. All he did was shrug. "I'm okay," he said. "Thank you for this. It's good, better than my dad makes…" He shoved another bite in his mouth.

She could see how hungry he was. At the same time, she didn't know what to do with Raymond's son. She reached for a glass in the cupboard and filled it with water from the tap, then slid it in front of him. "Not sure if there's anything I can say, Brady, to make this better for you…"

"Why would he do it?" he said.

For a second, she didn't know how to answer him, this teenage boy who seemed so very, very lost. "Do what, exactly, Brady? I'm not sure I'm clear on what you're asking. I take it we're talking about Raymond."

He just shrugged, not looking at her. There was awkwardness there.

She could hear Luke in the other room. What he was doing, she didn't know.

"You called him Raymond," Brady said. "He tells everyone to call him Ray. I didn't know he had a family before me. He said he left eighteen years ago. That's what he told me today. I'll be eighteen on October 16—so did I break up your family?"

For a second, she didn't know what to say. When she heard the door and voices, Raymond's voice, her heart thudded, and she couldn't move. She hadn't answered Brady, because how could she explain something that was beyond his control and couldn't have been his fault?

"Brady, whatever this is, none of it is on you," she said. "I don't know what your dad told you about what happened…"

Then Raymond was walking into her kitchen, Luke and Marcus behind him. Those O'Connell blue eyes completely unsettled her. It wasn't lost on her that the last time Raymond had been inside her house, it had been their house. They'd been a family, Iris and Raymond, and now he was someone else.

Brady didn't move from where he sat, holding the sandwich, gripping it so hard that the mayonnaise oozed out. He was still chewing, leaning on the counter with his elbows, refusing to look at his father. She recognized the teenage anger she'd experienced a time or two with her kids, each in his or her own way.

There it was again, the way Raymond looked at her. She couldn't remember him ever appearing uneasy, so damn confident. The moment stretched out, just the two of them. He didn't look away from her, but then he did, giving everything to his son, who was staring at that sandwich as if it held all the answers.

Awkwardness lingered.

"Why are you here?" Brady said, adding more of an edge to an already uncomfortable situation.

Marcus lingered in the background, looking as if he'd been pulled from bed. She wasn't sure why it bothered her that he'd shown up with Raymond. Evidently, his father had reached out to him.

"For you, son," Raymond said. "You can't be here. This isn't okay. Iris, I'm sorry."

All she could do was reach for the lid of the mayonnaise and put it back on. "Well, I'm sure you are, but still, this is where we are, isn't it?" She slid her gaze over to Brady, who was staring at her. She wondered if he expected her to throw him out. "Brady, I know you're angry, and you have a right to be…"

Brady shook his head and put his sandwich down on his plate. "I'm not going anywhere with him. Please tell him to go." He was looking right at her, and she felt torn. She didn't have to look over to Raymond to see that he wasn't going to take this lying down.

He stepped around the island, beside Iris, as Brady was refusing to look his way. Having him standing so close to her, being there, was exactly what she didn't want. Luke and Marcus were staring at them, and their expressions had her wanting to walk away. She had to stay, though, to be there for the young man in her kitchen, who'd had his world as he'd known it torn apart.

"Hey, don't talk as if I'm not even here," Raymond said. "I'm your father, and although you have a right to be upset, you don't get to pull a stunt like this. You have any idea how worried I was that something had happened to you?"

"I'm fine, as you can see," Brady snapped. She could feel Raymond tense.

"Okay, that's it, we're leaving," Raymond said. "Thank Iris for the sandwich. Let's go." He snapped his fingers and gestured sharply, but Brady simply slid off the stool, leaving his sandwich on the plate, and took a step over to Marcus and Luke, then fisted his hands as if ready to fight.

"No, I'm not going anywhere with you," he said. "You're such a liar. I hate you! How could you lie to me? I don't want to be with you right now. Iris, can I stay here?" He didn't wait for her to answer, though, now looking over to Marcus and Luke, almost as tall as them. "You're my brothers, right? Can I stay with one of you?"

Marcus rested a hand on his shoulder, and she knew what he was going to do, so she spoke without thinking.

"Brady, of course you can stay here," she said. And what about her granddaughter, who was over there almost every day?

"Maybe that's best for tonight," Marcus said, looking over to her, his hand still on Brady's shoulder.

"What are you doing?" Raymond said. She was forced to look up at him, standing so close to her.

"Look, considering the situation, Raymond, you have to understand that Brady needs some space," she said. "A night away will likely do you both good. You know well that I'm not willing to—"

"Can I talk to you a second, in private?" he said, cutting her off quite sharply, and somehow he maneuvered her out of the kitchen, his hand on her arm. "Brady, finish your sandwich, and then we're going," he called out over his shoulder as if he hadn't heard a word anyone said.

Once they were in the living room, he pulled his hand away and walked over to the window, looking out. It was something she noticed Luke doing a time or two when he was just back from one of his missions someplace overseas. Whatever it was he did, she had no idea. She knew only that he was in the special forces.

She glanced to the kitchen and could hear Luke, Marcus, and Brady talking, but she couldn't make out what they were saying. She took in the man she'd loved so deeply, whom she hadn't seen in nearly two decades. Here he was, in her living room, in the house he'd bought.

"Okay, Raymond, what is it?" she said. "It's late. Everyone has had a trying day, and evidently, Brady doesn't want to go home with you."

"He can't stay here," he said, the blue of his eyes flickering with something absolutely immovable. This was a man she didn't know, one who wasn't about to be convinced of anything.

"Of course he can," she said. "He'll be fine. He can stay in the girls' old room, where Alison and Eva sleep when they stay over. I'm sure a night away will have him thinking differently in the morning."

"You don't get it," Raymond said. "It's impossible. He can't stay."

Had she missed something? Even though this situation

was about as bad as it could get, she also knew it could've been so much worse, considering all the lies, the secrets, the truth of who he really was.

"You know what, Raymond? The fact is that you're the one who's going to have to go tonight. I'm sorry, but I'm on Brady's side here. You should be grateful that he showed up at my door instead of wandering around out there, lost. You should know that he's a great kid, too. Give him the night, and then you two can talk tomorrow."

He looked out the window again, then glanced back to the kitchen, where Marcus, Luke, and Brady were. Just something about it let her know, deep down, that he wasn't telling her something.

"What are you doing?" she said. "Why do you keep looking out the window?" She knew it had come out rather sharply.

He was standing right there in front of her. He pulled his hand over his chin, and the way he looked at her had the knot in her stomach tightening even more. "Not sure, just a feeling I have. Just so we're clear, I'm not walking out the door without Brady."

Had he always been this stubborn? Likely where her children all got it from. She let out a sigh, as he seemed to be considering something, then shook his head.

"Well, then I think we're at a standstill," she said, "because you're not dragging him out of here, by the way he's dug in. He's made his feelings clear. He's not a little kid. You can't just pick him up and make him leave."

"No, he's my son, Iris," Raymond said. "I hear you loud and clear on how I can't make him leave, but I'm not walking out the door without him."

For a second, she couldn't get her tongue to move. When she did, all that came out was "Excuse me?" She thought her voice squeaked.

"You heard me. Since he's hell-bent on staying here, then evidently I am, too."

There was no way, no goddamn way!

He slid off his jacket, tossed it on the chair, and gestured to the sofa. "I'll take the sofa. So do you want to tell them, or do you want me to?" he said, though it wasn't a question.

"I don't want you here, Raymond."

He pulled in a breath, and nothing in his expression told her he was willing to listen to reason. "I know you don't, and I understand, but this is happening. I'm staying, so either you tell them in the kitchen or I will, because that's the only choice I'm giving you."

Chapter Eight

Why was Raymond there now with Brady, anyway? That was the one question that had continued to plague her. He'd walked away all those years ago, so why had he come back?

Now he was in her living room, sleeping on the sofa, even though there were two single beds in the room where Brady slept. Evidently, Raymond staying with his son hadn't even been a consideration.

Their worlds had been completely turned upside down. When Raymond had told Luke, Marcus, and Brady that he was staying, the reaction hadn't been what she'd expected—because he was still there. How was this possible?

Now Iris was lying awake. It was just after two a.m., and she didn't hear a sound in the house, but she was staring into the dark, her mind going to the kinds of places she hadn't been in years, likely because the love of her life, who'd killed her hopes and dreams and brought her to her knees, was under her roof now. Maybe that was why sleep was eluding her.

"Damn you, Raymond, why?" she whispered.

She thought of Brady, who was looking to her for… what, exactly? She didn't have a clue.

She sat up and flicked on the bedside lamp, then tossed back the covers and put her feet on the cold floor, running her fingers through her short dark hair, tousled from sleep. She stood and reached for her silky housecoat on the back of her bathroom door, then pulled it on and pulled the tie at her waist to cover her short nightgown.

She pulled open the bedroom door, taking only a second to see the closed doors to the other rooms, Luke's and the one Brady was in. She strode down the darkened hall, the only light filtering out from her bedroom behind her.

She could hear the creak in the floorboards and continued into the kitchen just as a light flicked on above the stove. Her hand went to her chest as she jumped, and she took in Raymond standing there in his black jeans and T-shirt. She wondered whether he'd slept. As she took in his bare feet, she had to remind herself to breathe.

"What are you doing up?" he said in a way that reminded her of those last few nights, when he'd been up late, doing the kinds of things she still didn't understand. After that, she hadn't seen him again, not until now, over eighteen years later.

"Well, I couldn't sleep"—she gestured to the cupboard —"so I thought a glass of water would help."

He pulled open the cupboard and reached for a glass, then held it out to her. He waited and then gestured. "Well, do you want it, or should we just stand here? Or is this about something else entirely, and you wanted an excuse to come out here?"

She forced herself to take a step and then another, then reached for the glass he was holding, wondering when he'd become such an asshole. "You seem to forget, Raymond, that you're the intruder. You shouldn't even be here. I don't get you. Why are you even here?"

He gestured to the sink when she just stood there. "So this isn't about a glass of water, then? Just say so, Iris. I'm not in the mood to play detective about why you're out here when you should be sleeping."

Just looking at him, she could see such arrogance. All she could do was make a rude noise and lift the tap to fill a glass of water that she didn't really want. She lifted it to her lips and took a swallow, seeing his image reflected in the kitchen window, and she thought he stifled a smile.

"Well, that's one way to handle it," he said. "But it seems you have something on your mind, Iris, so just ask already."

Had he always been like this, so abrupt and dismissive? Maybe, if she thought only about how he had been at the end, and maybe that was why she couldn't figure out why he'd come back.

"I don't understand why you're here in Livingston, Raymond. You were here before the charges against me, and yes, you fixed the situation, sort of, but you were responsible for it all, anyway. You were living here before. I don't understand why. Why come back here? Then there's Brady. You played with fire, and my granddaughter and Brady are the ones getting burned. You had to know something like this could happen." She rested the still full glass on the counter and turned to him, hearing how quiet the house was with everyone asleep. Morning was still a long way off.

"So you want to fight," he said, and it took everything in her not to fist her hands. Just being around him was stirring feelings she didn't want to feel.

"No, Raymond, I don't want to fight with you, but here

you are, standing in the kitchen of my house, not answering my questions…"

"You mean our house, the house I bought."

She angled her head. How could she have forgotten how quick he was? She'd never been able to win a verbal sparring match with him. Raymond just had the ability to think fast on his feet in a way she never had.

"Wow, really, so this is suddenly your house?" she said sharply, then turned to the hallway, wondering whether anyone had heard. She forced herself to pull in a breath as she reminded herself he had no rights there. Then she lifted her gaze to him, again refusing to look away.

He kept looking out the window, then strode away, back into the living room, barefoot, appearing too much at home. How could this be so easy for him?

It was pure instinct to just follow him, mainly because she could feel the possibility of him steamrolling right over her, and that wasn't happening. How could she have forgotten how strong minded he was, how he would pick and choose what to answer?

"I won't be ignored or dismissed, Raymond," she said. "You seem to not want to answer, but I'm going to ask you again: Why did you show up here and then move into a house so close to me? I need to know. You're suddenly in our lives when you were the one who walked out on us. You had so many years when you could've reached out, but here you are now."

He was at the living room window now, staring out. Only a trickle of streetlight filled the room, and she took in the sofa, on which sat the blanket, still folded, and pillow Luke had tossed him. He let the sheers fall back and stepped away, over to her.

"You want the truth?"

"Please," she said, feeling the sarcasm and wondering if he'd answer.

"To see the kids, our kids, for myself, in person. Yes, Iris, I may have left, but I've watched all of you from a distance for years—you, the kids and the trouble they got in. I saw that you never dated again. Leaving and watching was the only way I could be sure nothing bad touched you, but just because I walked away, that didn't mean I wasn't responsible for you. You're right that I knew I was playing with fire, coming back here, but I did it anyway. You did a great job with the kids."

Was she supposed to take that as a compliment? She pulled her arms across her chest, feeling the carpet beneath her feet. Raymond didn't look away. It was unnerving, and she was already anticipating the moment he'd be gone with Brady and she'd never see him again.

"I did all I could do," she said. "You expect me to say thank you? Because I won't. Raising six kids alone was the hardest thing I did, but I did it, yet here you are, saying you've been watching the kids. I don't get you. I don't get any of this."

He said nothing, as if the silence wasn't awkward to him at all.

"I don't understand what you said to Marcus and Luke, either," she said. "Why are they suddenly okay with you staying here?"

She had expected Luke to toss his dad out, but he hadn't, and Marcus had simply asked her if she would be okay before he left. Like, what the hell was that?

"It's not a big deal, Iris. The only one who seems to have an issue with it is you. Yes, we should've been gone, but that decision was taken from my hands because my son has suddenly discovered his voice and doesn't want to leave. We stayed too long. The reasons I left you years ago still apply, Iris. We can't stay. We have to keep moving…"

"Now hang on a second, here," she said, stepping closer to him, mindful to keep her voice low. "I thought you left years ago because you're not really Raymond O'Connell, and those men who showed up, looking for you, were putting us all in danger. Look at what happened, what you put me through and set in motion. Even though you left eighteen years ago—well, nineteen, actually, this coming November—here we are, with the same issues affecting young Brady. He's eighteen, or almost, so who was Brady's mother, the woman you left me for? Why don't we just put it all out on the table, Raymond, or whatever your name is, all the lies and more lies…"

She hadn't meant to ask, but the danger that seemed to follow Raymond was morphing into something far more complex. He had another family. Then there was the one question she'd never really asked: Who was Raymond O'Connell, really? Right now, she realized that although she'd told herself for years that knowing wouldn't matter, she wanted to know. No, she needed to know.

"I never left you for Nancy," he said.

Okay, maybe she hadn't wanted to know her name. Him just saying another woman's name brought an ache to her gut. It shouldn't have bothered her the way it did.

"Really? Yet you left me and were with someone else, Brady's mother. You sure didn't wait long, now, did you?"

He pulled in a breath, looked away, and shook his head. "I don't know what you expect me to say, Iris. Leaving you and the kids wasn't something I wanted, but it was something that had to happen because of the danger I brought to the doorstep. Nancy wasn't who you think she was."

Had he always talked in riddles?

She made a face. "Really? Then tell me who she was," she said, though she wondered whether he'd say anything, considering how tight-lipped he'd become.

He stared long and hard down at her and took a step closer, so close that she could feel his heat. She could feel all of him and had to fight the urge to step away. "You really want to know?" he said. "Nancy was with the CIA here, in the States. I slept with her so she wouldn't see other things that could get me caught after I left you, considering questions had been raised, and no one had any idea who I was working for. In truth, Mossad had me working for the CIA so that I could report to them exactly what was going on in this government. Then you know what happened. Things got complicated because I fell in love with you, and you'd gone from just a cover to something more. Then there were our kids. The minute Mossad figured out I was no longer a team player and had likely switched sides, they showed up, looking for me. Those are the kinds of people who would've hurt you and the kids. So yes, I had left you, but Nancy wasn't the love of my life. That was you. Having Brady was never the plan, either, but she was killed in an accident, and that forced me to make some hard choices. I left the CIA and Mossad, but once you're an agency man, even after you leave, you always end up looking over your shoulder because the things you did could still come back on you. There are some bad people out there, Iris, and me being here now could bring them back again. Is that what you want?"

When he stepped away, back to the window, looking out, she realized what he was doing. "So that's why you keep doing that," she said, gesturing.

He let the curtain fall and strode back to her. "You mean watching, keeping an eye out? Yeah, Iris, it is, because someone needs to. Anything else?"

She nodded. "As a matter of fact, I think I have a right to know who you really are, your real name. Is it David?"

He just shook his head. "I go by Ray now. I know what you're talking about, but David ceased to exist the day he met you, Iris. I have no plans to ever be him again. You should go to bed."

Just the way he said it was so familiar, as was the way he took another step, closer. It was too much like she remembered. As he slid his hand under her chin, her heart kicked up a beat. His was a touch she'd never expected to feel again.

She stepped back and turned her head, feeling the cool air, and heard him sigh. "Goodnight, Raymond," she whispered, then stepped away, back to the kitchen. At first, all he did was incline his head.

"Iris," he called out.

She rested her hand in the kitchen archway as she turned back to him, but she didn't say anything.

"Hurting you is the biggest regret of my life," he said.

What could she say to that?

"Is this where I'm supposed to say it's okay?"

He didn't look away. "No, it's not okay."

She tapped the door frame. "Goodnight," she said again, but this time, she made herself turn from him. She flicked off the light in the kitchen. When she turned back, he was looking out the window again.

Chapter Nine

Raymond heard something.

As he opened his eyes, he sat up from where he must have fallen asleep in the easy chair. The sun was up, and Luke was walking his way, wearing a wrinkled orange T-shirt and blue jeans and holding two coffees.

"So you stayed up all night." Luke offered the steaming mug, taking in the still folded blanket at the end of the sofa with a pillow on top. "Don't know how you take it, so you're getting it black."

Raymond reached for the mug, unsure of what to make of the expression on his son's face. He took a welcome swallow, feeling the ache from lack of sleep. "It's fine. Appreciate it."

"Heard you and Mom out here last night, arguing."

"Sorry. Do you want me to say I didn't plan on it? I didn't expect to find myself here, camping out. Your mom is a little thrown, and of course she wants answers I can't really give her…"

"Answers you don't want to give her, is what you're really saying." Luke walked over to the window and moved the sheer curtains aside, glancing out, looking around, something he'd never expected one of his kids to do.

"So you decided to join the special forces," Raymond said. "What's your team again, the Wardogs?"

Luke didn't pull his gaze from the window, taking a swallow of his coffee. Raymond knew his son's special forces team didn't exist on paper. The 77th Operational Delta did the kinds of things for their country that Raymond knew all too well. He wondered if his son had ever been asked to do the things he had done.

"Is this what you did with Mom?" Luke said. "It's a wonder she didn't want to kill you, figuratively speaking. She'd never let any of us get away with that, flipping a conversation by asking a question or changing the subject. I get that you don't want to talk about Mom, but you want to drop hints that you know everything about me and what I do, knowing I can't and won't talk about it? That leaves us with what subject—Brady, or the fact that you messed around with another woman and left a posse of kids and a wife to fend for ourselves? You brought a whole shitload of trouble down on Mom, but not to worry, Pops: There's not a chance in hell that we're about to let you walk in here and mess with her. You had your fun, camping out for the night, keeping watch for the boogie man, but what's the plan now? Let's get into the nitty gritty of this shit. It's just you and me here. No one else is up. Let's get real and down to it."

Raymond realized that Luke understood who he was, and maybe he could also understand why he couldn't stay in the place where his fantasy life had been snatched away. He was well aware of how carefully he'd have to tread.

"You think I chose this life?" he said. He didn't pull his gaze at first, but then he did, staring into his mug of coffee before lifting it and taking another swallow. Luke didn't do the normal things most people did. He knew his son had the kind of training that had made him see the dirty side of people, what went on behind the scenes, which the average person didn't know. Lies, scandal, deceit.

"Didn't you? So tell me, who was your contact in the CIA? You had to know I was looking for anything on you. How is it that someone could just disappear? You can't, not unless you don't really exist and are working for an agency that knows how to make it happen. I figured that out from all the dead ends."

It seemed his son wanted to cut right to the heart of it.

"You keep sitting there, saying nothing," Luke continued. "Come on, Pops. Who are you protecting? If not the CIA, who is it? Another country, agency? Which one? You're not answering, but you have a lot to answer for, considering what happened to Mom. Let's talk about the men who showed up. Mom killed one. I still remember what she said. Karen, Suzanne, Ryan, and Owen wouldn't have any idea, but maybe Marcus has some. Jack definitely knows more than I'm comfortable with. I know that whatever brought them here, Mom said she knew they'd hurt us kids without a second thought. They'd have done so much worse because of whatever you were mixed up in. Maybe it's not even government. Some crime syndicate, organization, corporation…?"

"You don't stop, do you?" Raymond finally cut him off, seeing how Luke was digging and digging and would keep at him until he gave him something. "You may not want the answers I have to give."

"Oh, I guarantee that part's true, but you're going to tell me anyhow. Why Mom?"

"What do you mean?"

"I think you know that Raymond O'Connell didn't exist until he met Iris. You had suddenly shown up in

Livingston and were working for the railroad, doing what, exactly? Some cover. That means you had an order from some government to set up a new life, to put yourself in a position that would give you a cover, but something went wrong. Am I close?"

He pulled in a breath, feeling his chest ache. He'd had to tell himself that falling in love was something he would never do, could never do. Boy, had he been wrong. Apparently, he was human after all.

"I was an agent for Mossad," he said, "pulled from the streets when I was sixteen, in trouble. First, I was an informant, but then the Israelis wanted boots on the ground to keep tabs on their allies. I was only one of many. It would be easier to hide in the city, but a job was arranged with the railroad here in Livingston so I could blend in. I met your mother, married her, had weekends and overnight trips away for jobs. I was meeting a team that was already here, taking care of a problem, gathering intelligence, not much different than what you do, only when needed. You know, you're following orders, but soon you find yourself on the dirty side of government business. Then something happened." He stopped talking, because there were things he knew he couldn't share and had never talked about, things that had changed the course of everything.

"So you were, what, a sleeper agent? I kind of figured it was something like that."

"Then you know that I was to fit in and have a normal life until I was issued an order by my country. I was lulled into the dream here, barely hearing from them for five years. Then there were just one or two things to be taken care of here and there. The overnight trips that had been so infrequent in the beginning happened more and more often. The world stage had changed, and my country was reaching out. You would understand clearly from your side of things, because we're not that different. You just have a different flag behind you."

"Whoa, hang on there, Pops. If you're trying to say we're alike, then you're way off target."

"Oh, you're very wrong there. I know what you do." Raymond cut him off. "You just haven't been forced to walk away from your family, this family."

Luke said nothing else, but Raymond could see he'd hit a nerve.

"We were ordered to take care of someone who'd become a problem. With the rise in conflict on the world stage after the terrorist attacks, wars were breaking out, and alliances were being re-evaluated. My role had gone past gathering information and sending it back. We were ordered to take out an asset. Was that the first time?" He just shook his head, seeing faces that still haunted him. "I don't need to explain to you that you don't question orders, but I made that mistake. I started asking questions—who, and why? Why did this asset, who turned out to be a decorated war veteran, have to be taken out? He was a black man from rural Georgia, a man with a wife and a mentally challenged son. Orders were given to kill him and make it look as if the son had done it. You know how easy it is to manipulate and stage a crime scene, especially in a small rural town where the only evidence used is what the local law enforcement see in front of them. Well, I had a problem with it."

Luke had gone quiet. "So what did you do?"

What the hell was he supposed to say to that? That was the first time he'd had any idea of the kind of monster he was. "It wasn't exactly timely for me to suddenly choose to have a conscience, all because innocent people were getting caught in the crossfire, pissing off the wrong person in the wrong government."

His team were the same men who had come looking for him after he walked away from the job and disobeyed orders. How could he have expected to go on and not suddenly find himself hunted?

"They killed him anyway, didn't they?" Luke said.

He didn't think he'd ever get the image out of his head, or the evidence they'd planted at the scene. He continued: "I found myself duct taped and tucked in a trunk, but I managed to get out, hearing the sirens and knowing the police would find prints on a gun lying in the bedroom of a severely mentally challenged young black man, with his parents both dead in their bed. He'd likely have been sitting on death row and wouldn't understand how or what had happened. They were coming out the back, but I snuck in after them and took the gun from where it had been planted. I made a call to 911 on my burner as I was walking away, saying I heard shots fired and had spotted two white men sneaking out of the house. I gave the descriptions of the two from my team, Ivan Dobson and Saul Gusterson—not their real names, of course. Ivan was the man your mom killed. She stabbed him. Saul was the one who helped me drag his body out of there and bury it.

"At that point, their descriptions were in the system in relation to a murder that had gone unsolved. I'd screwed them, so I had a target on me. It wasn't the kind of embarrassment my country wanted. My next call after the police was to a woman I knew, Nancy Baker, with the CIA. I had known her for years. She knew who I was, and I knew who she was and what she did. Did I cross over?" He shook his head, still remembering her eyes, the fun, the flirtation, right before she could turn into the same kind of person he was. "I was recruited. I was her recruit, but leaving Mossad wasn't that easy, and she and I both knew it wouldn't be. That last job was eighteen months before they showed up at the house when you all were in bed. There had been a change in director at Israel's central intelligence agency, and his first order of business was cleaning up loose ends. I was very much the kind of problem he needed taken care of."

Luke only shook his head, then leaned forward. "Well, the pieces are starting to fall into place. So, what, they showed up and tried to get you to go back?"

"They offered me a chance to start over, return to Israel, share everything, be debriefed, and rectify my wrongs, but what they were doing was rounding me up. I'd have been on a plane, and the minute I stepped off, I'd have been charged with treason. I'd be interrogated fully, and they'd drag from me every single thing I had learned since joining the CIA."

"You mean you'd be tortured," Luke cut in.

He knew his son would know all the intimate details of what really went on behind the scenes. "You can call it whatever you want, but they'd do whatever they had to do to make sure they got everything or that I was dead. They needed me to leave willingly, but your mother figured out how bad they were when she walked in. That was the kind of evil I had worked with. I'd never considered how a person could become so cold and remorseless. It hadn't taken long for them to figure out that Iris and you all were my Achilles' heel. I couldn't hide that. Would they have taken you, all of you, and killed you? I think you know well what they'd have done, and we were fast slipping into that dangerous territory. They'd have made me watch, and your mother, too. They'd likely have started with one of you boys, then gone right to Suzanne, the youngest girl. What they'd have done to her, to each of you..." He stopped talking. He knew that the screams, the horror, would have made him agree to anything to get them to stop. He'd have made anything up, signed anything, begged and pleaded.

Luke shut his eyes and lifted his thumb and forefinger to the bridge of his nose, then glanced off to the side. Raymond knew he was trying to understand what he was saying, but he wondered whether Luke had ever been in the same position that Ivan and Saul had.

"So why leave?" Luke said. "I don't understand."

"Really, you don't get that they weren't taking no for an answer? The new director was still flexing his power, and the justifications he gave to the prime minister for taking me out would've been distorted. You know that's how it works. The truth is the spin they put on it. Leaders of countries know when they're being lied to, but maybe that's how they sleep at night. Not knowing the truth is better for them. I knew I had to leave, because after we buried Ivan, I told Saul I was going right to the CIA, and if something happened to my family, to Iris, to any of you, I'd share everything I knew. I'd been smart enough to copy records for every job, the details of who, what, and why, everything that could embarrass a country if it got out in the world. I told him to pass that message on. I sent the director a copy of what I had, and I said the originals would go to the CIA if something were to happen to me. It would be automatic."

Having his son staring back at him was like looking in a mirror. Luke had the same knowing, the same understanding, having seen the same darkness.

"So Nancy was Brady's mother?" Luke said.

He only nodded. He'd never expected her to come to him where he'd been watching his family from afar.

"She mean anything to you, or was she just a cover, too? You said she died."

What was he supposed to say? Nancy had saved his ass,

but she didn't know everything. He'd slept with her so she wouldn't see everything he'd been hiding. She was too good at what she did. "I cared for her, but that's it. The love of my life was someone I couldn't have in my life anymore. You should know that Nancy and I were never together aside from a few times, and it was after I left you all. We never had a relationship other than business, sex. I found out about Brady after she was killed."

"She died in a car accident?" Luke said.

Raymond shook his head. "So they said…"

He heard a creak and turned quickly in his chair to see Brady standing there in the same clothes he had worn the day before, his hair sticking up. He didn't have a clue how much his son had heard. Careless was something Raymond never was. He stood up from his chair. "You're awake," he said.

Brady stared at him long and hard, then turned and started to walk away.

"Brady, don't walk away when I'm talking—"

"So my mother meant nothing to you?" Brady snapped. Evidently, he'd heard something.

"Look, I don't know what you heard, but some things are complicated."

Brady was clearly not ready to listen to anything he had to say. He was shaking his head, looking over to Luke and then back to him. "Well, that's the thing, Dad: Everything always was complicated with you. 'It's complicated, Brady.' Isn't that what you always said? I guess now things are starting to make sense. I don't understand, though. Why bother with me? You already had another family."

Okay, so he hadn't heard everything. Raymond sighed. "Because you are my family. It doesn't matter what your mom and I were to each other. You're my son."

Brady said nothing, then slid his gaze over to Luke. "I'm going to take a shower," he said.

Luke gestured toward the bathroom down the hall and stood up. "Go on, kid," he said. "Just don't use all the hot water."

Then Brady walked away, and, not for the first time in his life, Raymond felt he was pedaling backwards up a hill, going nowhere.

"I'll have him out of here after he showers," he said.

An odd smile touched his son's lips. "Yeah, I don't think that's happening anytime soon. You may want to go to Plan B, and when that doesn't work, try telling him the truth, because maybe then you might get him to listen."

Chapter Ten

As Iris opened her eyes, the sun streamed through the blinds. She took in her closed bedroom door and the clock, seeing that it was after nine, but the quiet of the house bothered her. When she blinked again, she remembered that not only Brady was there but also Raymond. Her life, her house, her privacy had been turned upside down, invaded by a man who had no right to destroy any part of the new life she'd created for herself and her family.

The way he'd touched her, the way he'd talked to her, the way he'd looked at her…

No more! She wouldn't let him stay.

She took her time showering and then pulled on yoga pants and a loose cream shirt. Then she pulled open her door and stepped out, expecting something but hearing nothing. Maybe he was gone.

"Yay!" she said to herself, though not feeling the happy relief she'd hoped for.

As she stepped into the empty kitchen, she spotted the

coffeemaker with a full pot—freshly made, apparently, based on the timer. She pulled a mug from the cupboard and reached for the carafe to pour herself some.

"So you're finally up."

She damn near dropped the carafe, spilling some on the counter, as she jumped. Her heart zigged and her stomach zagged, and she turned, taking in Raymond, put together, tidy, cleaned up. He had changed into blue jeans and a black long-sleeved shirt, but he hadn't shaved. His day-old whiskers were tinged with dark gray, only adding to his attractiveness.

"Sorry," he said. "Didn't mean to scare you."

He didn't move from where he leaned in the doorway —tall, too handsome for his own good and for her. Looking at him, she could see how her sons had grown too much into his image. She forced herself to swallow.

"Why are you still here?" she said. "And where're Luke and Brady?"

Maybe because of the way he was looking at her, as if he could see how he was affecting her, she had to look away. She settled the coffeepot back on the burner and then reached for the sponge in the sink to wipe up the spill on the counter. Then she lifted her mug and turned, because he still hadn't answered. Then he did.

"Luke took Brady back to the house to get a change of clothes after I got back. It seems my son would rather spend time with anyone but me. He's still angry. I haven't had a chance to sit him down and talk. Luke thought it would be best if he talked to him instead to get a feel for where his head is at."

She took a swallow of the dark brew and could feel the awkwardness, considering how he kept looking at her.

"I guess I didn't like how we left it last night," he said. "In fact, Luke insisted I talk to you about some things."

She didn't know why, but she found herself squeezing her mug, feeling the burn. Her muscles pulled across her shoulders with the kind of tension that had become her constant companion as of late. "And why would Luke want you talking to me? This was supposed to be just for the night. Brady was upset, and I get that, but now you're still here, and you're saying Brady is with Luke? This is becoming complicated, Raymond. You should be gone already."

She pulled her gaze away, back to her coffee, and took another swallow as she leaned against the sink. Evidently, it was just them in the house, alone, her and a man she'd never expected to see again.

She didn't understand why he was looking at her the way he was. It made her damned uncomfortable. Then he glanced away, seeming to consider something, and held his hand out to her. What the hell was he doing?

"Come with me, and let's go sit down," he said.

She wondered if the panic licking at the back of her throat showed on her face as he stood there, his hand still held out. Was he crazy? There was no way she was letting him touch her ever again.

"Here's good," she said, with the island between them. He nodded and dropped his hand, then firmed his lips as if annoyed. Good. Maybe now he would leave.

"I wanted to talk to you about some things you don't know but should, in all fairness to you. This has come up because Brady overheard me talking with Luke early this morning."

She knew she wasn't going to like this. "Oh," she said. What would it be? Was it about where he was going, who he really was, how he'd never loved her? Yeah, she didn't want to know.

"First, it's about Brady's mother," he said. "You should know we were never involved in the way you thought."

Now her heartbeat kicked up, and she had to fight the urge to roll her shoulders. "I have no idea what you're trying to say, Raymond. Does it matter how you were involved? You were involved. Sure, it was after you left, as you pointed out, but it seems you jumped right into another bed. So after all these years, does it matter? No." She forced a swallow and took in the odd smile that touched his lips.

"Well, then I guess you're better than me, Iris, because it would have bothered me. If it were you with another man, I'd probably have killed him. But I'm glad you're okay with it. In all honesty, I didn't even know about Brady until after his mother died," he said, and she wished he'd stop talking.

"And you told Luke about all this, and he wanted you to tell me?" she said. Now she'd be having a word with Luke, because there was a point where this became about digging the knife in deeper, and that was the kind of pain she wasn't into. She shook her head.

Raymond walked closer to her and rested his hand on the fridge, taking it in. "Didn't I buy this one?" he said, actually running his hand over the fridge, then gave everything to her in that one look. Seriously?

"Who cares about the fridge?" she said. "Yes, I'm sure it's the one you bought—evidently a good choice, because it still works. But get to it already, Raymond, because I don't like these games." She had to pull in another breath because of how sharply her words had come out. Her heartbeat kicked up another notch.

"Luke wanted me to tell you everything. He seemed to think it would matter. Brady was two when Nancy died, and Nancy had no family to speak of. I received a call from a friend of hers. She had apparently left word to contact me if something happened to her. Nancy and I were together after I left you. It wasn't planned, and it was meaningless, just two people, sex and nothing else. It would never have happened again. I knew her because I worked with her, in a way. The car accident she died in was conveniently made to look like a hit and run. I knew then that someone had figured it out. When I met Brady, I took him and moved him, knowing I didn't have a handle on my troubles anymore. Looking over my shoulder had become constant, but after that, I made sure not to stay in one place too long."

"And now here you are. Am I supposed to thank you for just sleeping with her, having a kid, and it not meaning anything? There really is a difference between men and women. So Brady overheard this, did he? Hmm, I wonder why he'd be upset, Raymond." Even she could hear the sarcasm dripping from her words as she thought of who he was and wasn't.

Raymond O'Connell. The name kept going through her mind.

"If you're trying to say I screwed up, you've made your point. I didn't know Brady was standing there. He took whatever he heard out of context, and he's probably making a ton of assumptions, way more than I'm comfortable with, considering I've controlled the narrative of what he knew. You should know I assumed his mom's last name, Baker. He's going to have a ton of questions about that, as well. He has no idea what I do or did. The deal that I made to stay on US soil has me reporting to a friend of Nancy's at the CIA, the one who called me to let me know Luke was looking for me."

All of this was coming full circle in a way she didn't want. She forced herself to pull in a breath. "I don't know what to say. Okay, so you've told me. Consider yourself off the hook for having to explain anything else, but don't expect me to say thank you. If that's why you're still here…"

He didn't smile and didn't look away as he crossed his arms, looking out the kitchen window, past her, and then back to her again. "No, I'm still here because Brady won't leave. I left you and the kids to protect you, but when I went public to the Feds and the DA here, I put a spotlight on you once again, all of you, the kids."

"What are you saying?" She rested her mug on the counter.

"I'm saying I'm not going anywhere. I can't. The situation with Brady has changed because he knows a truth I never wanted him to know. I figured I was protecting all of you, except now I realize I was protecting no one. My plan wasn't really a plan. I was just staying one step ahead of something the average person has no idea about."

"So you're staying in Livingston," she said. No, this couldn't be happening.

He didn't nod and didn't look away. "Well, that would be part of it." He uncrossed his arms and took another step closer to her, then rested his hand on the counter beside her. "The other part is that I'm not leaving this house. I left you because I thought that was the only way to protect you and the kids, but now the only way I can do it is to stay right here, with Brady."

She had to remind herself to breathe. "You're not staying here, Raymond. There's no way…"

He was standing right in front of her, too close for comfort. "Well, that's where you're wrong, Iris. I am staying. I'm not leaving."

"For how long?" she snapped.

He just shook his head. "No idea. A while, until I know with certainty that you're safe, that the kids are safe, that no one else is coming out of the shadows for any of us. Until Brady listens to reason. Take your pick."

She was shaking her head, too. "No, absolutely not. I can't make you leave Livingston, but you have a house. You can go back there. You're not staying here. The kids are all coming over tonight, and you're not going to be here. You can't just decide to walk back into our lives and expect me to be okay with this, any of this."

He smiled, arrogant, cocky, and stepped back again. "Iris, you don't have to be okay with it. It's good that the kids are coming over. I'll have to tell everyone only once, and they'll understand. Hear me, Iris: I'm not leaving. I'll sleep on the sofa. I'll figure things out with Brady and make it right with the kids, and then…"

She just stared in horror, because this couldn't be happening. "The kids will make you leave," she said. "I'll ask them to make you."

That odd smile touched his lips again, and he stepped back, the arrogant light flickering in those O'Connell blue eyes. She could feel the fire burning like a knot in her stomach, furious, angry.

"We'll see about that," he said, then jutted his chin at her. "Oh, and the security system Luke installed? Short of putting bars on the windows, it isn't going to keep out anyone, at least not the kinds of people who need to be kept out. I plan on adding a few things, a new front door, and cutting down the bushes at the side of the house…"

Then he was out the back door, still talking, and all she could think was that this man, who'd turned her life upside down and abandoned her and her children, had just walked back in the same way he'd left, and he was talking as if he had every right to do so.

Well, that was where he was wrong, and Iris had every intention of making sure he understood how far he'd over-stepped her boundaries.

Chapter Eleven

He knew Iris was angry—no, furious, as she sat out back. That she'd gone out of her way all day to avoid him in a house far too small for them to avoid each other was a feat that had not gone unnoticed. Also out back was Brady, sitting in a lawn chair, sulking, with Alison across from him, as well as little Eva, Charlotte, Jenny, and Tessa.

Raymond was standing in the living room in a circle with his grown sons, Owen, Ryan, and Marcus, with Luke lingering in the background, everyone staring at him. This was where he needed to come clean, except he was still missing Karen and Suzanne and their respective partners, whom he wanted to look in the eye, face to face, to be sure they were who he'd seen on paper.

"How is this okay?" Ryan finally said. "I don't even know where to begin, considering you basically ruined mine and my wife's wedding by showing up yesterday, of all days…"

Owen responded on cue by making a rude noise. Yeah, he evidently had way more of a chip on his shoulder than anyone else.

"Ryan, I'm sorry," Raymond said. "Yesterday was unavoidable. If I could go back…"

"Seriously, you're doing this now?" Owen said, cutting him off and lifting his hands as if ready to fight. In fact, it was as if he wanted a fight.

"No, in all fairness, if I could go back in time, that's not what I'd change. But again, Ryan, I'm sorry about yesterday. Today, as I said to your mother, I wanted to talk to you, all of you. It's only fair."

"Fair!" Owen cut in again, pulling his hands back out from where he'd jammed them in his pockets. His firstborn had evidently already made up his mind, and Raymond wondered how much he'd actually listen to.

He could see that Marcus was having a lot of trouble, too. He hadn't said anything to him since walking into the house with Charlotte and Eva and heading right for his mother. Right, hadn't Marcus always been his mother's son?

"Okay, poor choice of words," Raymond said. "I've already talked with Luke this morning. Brady, as you know, is outside. I'd like to wait until Karen and Suzanne get here. They are coming, right?"

He didn't know why he found himself looking to Luke, but just then, he heard a car door and then another. He stepped over to the window and pulled the sheers back to see his little Karen, all grown up, holding the hand of her husband, Jack. Then there was Suzanne, and that had to be the deputy boyfriend—what was his name…Harold?

He stepped back. No one had said anything, but Owen and Ryan still appeared puzzled, and Luke had crossed his arms and was leaning against the wall, and he jutted his chin toward the door just as it opened.

"Hey, everyone," Karen started, all smiles. She wore heels and a dress, her vibrant red hair pulled up in a messy bun. She stopped as her gaze fell totally and completely on him, her expression much like it had been the day before.

"What's going on?" Suzanne said as she appeared behind her. She was tall and slim, kind of a tomboy, he thought. She really did look just like his mother, her grandmother.

"Dad…" Karen said, her voice soft and filled with emotion. Suzanne didn't say a word.

"Hey, darlin'." He took a step toward the two, but Jack stepped around Karen, toward him.

"I'm Jack Curtis, Karen's husband," he said, not holding out his hand. He had blue eyes and was shorter than Raymond, but he didn't seem to hesitate. Maybe there was something about him that he could like.

"Raymond," was all he said in reply.

Still by the door, Harold had his hand on Suzanne, who was staring at him, no smile, no amusement, no curiosity. It took him a second to get past the tightness in his chest at being in the same room as his grown children, something he'd never expected to happen, even though he knew not everyone was happy he was there.

"So you're probably all wondering why I'm here," he said. "Suzanne, Karen, come on down here." He gestured to the living room before pinching the bridge of his nose to get his thoughts together, something he couldn't remember ever having had such trouble with.

"Well, let's hear it," Owen said. "Karen and Suzanne are here, so spit it out, and then you can get the hell out of here."

Ryan was pissed off, too, based on his expression, but Raymond could see he was likely more thrown than anything. Marcus, meanwhile, was working a piece of gum, dressed in all navy blue, a faded T-shirt, blue jeans, nothing to resemble the cop he was.

"Owen, I get it. You're pissed off. You have every right to be."

"Shit…" was all Owen muttered under his breath.

He took in how close Suzanne was standing to Karen, shell-shocked, confused. She was the baby and had been so much younger than the others when he left. He didn't have a clue what she was thinking, by the way she was staring at him.

"Why don't you just cut to it?" Marcus said. "Why are you here? I think we'd all like to know. I get that you stayed here last night because of Brady, but why are you still here? I mean, can you even imagine how Mom is feeling right now? Actually, she wants you gone." He uncrossed one of his arms and gestured out back before crossing them again.

"Oh, I'm sure she does," Raymond said. "What I want to say is that keeping the secret about who I am and why I had to leave eighteen years ago is kind of pointless now."

Then there was silence. Luke stared at him long and hard, his brows raised, because he knew exactly what Raymond had been a part of.

"Let me ask you this," Jack said. "You being back, does it put a target on my wife, on Iris, on anyone here?"

It took Raymond a second to realize Jack likely knew way more than he was comfortable with. "That's why I'm here with Brady," Raymond explained. "I wanted to move us back to the shadows, where we've lived, where I've raised him, but after coming forward for your mom, I'm afraid the spotlight is now shining on this family, on everyone. The DA has made it worse. I spent some time considering a lot of things today. You already know, I'm pretty sure, that Raymond O'Connell didn't exist until thirty-five years ago. He met a gorgeous woman and married her. I worked for another government, was planted here, and made a deal with a US government official, a woman named Nancy Baker, who was Brady's mother…"

Ryan swore, and Suzanne and Karen gasped. He took in the shock on their faces. Luke lingering in the background, saying nothing.

"Who the hell are you, then?" Owen snapped, appearing confused, angry. "I mean, if you're not Raymond O'Connell, then what does that make us?"

He couldn't help but glance at Jack, who was standing with his arms crossed. From his expression, he was positive the man understood without him having to elaborate. He looked down and shook his head, then lifted it and gave him everything. "Which government?" was all he asked.

"Israel, but we parted ways," Raymond said, then stopped before he said anything more. What he'd shared with Luke that morning was something he didn't want in anyone else's head.

"What the hell does 'parted ways' mean? Was there a disagreement?" Ryan asked. Karen and Suzanne were still just staring at him, and he could see they didn't have a clue what to say.

"It means he wouldn't do someone's dirty work," Luke said, and everyone turned to him. "It means he developed a conscience and walked away. There are some things you don't need to know, but basically, he pissed off the wrong people and made a deal to stay here. It's just that once you're on a hit list, you always have to watch over your shoulder. The man Mom killed, you all know, was here to bring our father back to Israel because he posed a problem for national security. He left to protect us, all of us—so dial back some of your outrage, Owen. At the same time, walking in here like you've done, Pops, do you have any idea who's watching?"

What could he say? He was operating on next to no

sleep, but he'd gone days without before. "Oh, someone definitely is. This quiet scares the hell out of me." He took in eight pairs of eyes, all giving him everything now, likely because he'd said the one thing he hadn't wanted to admit to himself. "When I left eighteen years ago, it was to keep you all safe, yes. I stayed away, made a deal with the CIA. I gave them information about my country, but one of the smartest things I did was to keep copies of everything I had been ordered to do, with a list of names of all the sleeper agents still in this country, to be sent to my contact in the CIA. What you don't know, Luke, is that my contact is the boss of someone you work with."

"God damn!" Luke snapped. "I knew there was something there. I knew I was being played, looking for you, when all that was there was a big black hole. I never found out from you this morning, but the Raymond O'Connell who was living in Wisconsin…"

He could see the confusion on his other children's faces. Apparently, they weren't in the loop with Luke, but then, he couldn't see his son sharing anything of his national security business. That was knowledge he would take to his grave.

"That was a coincidence," Raymond said. "I took Nancy's last name, Baker. I did know you were looking, though. I knew what each of you was doing. I may have left eighteen years ago, but that didn't mean I wasn't watching over you. Suzanne, you never would've gotten anywhere with the shitheads who've controlled that fire department since before I was here. They screwed you, but you'll find something else. Until there's a change at the top, with the family that has controlled it, you won't be welcome. Karen, you've done well, my darling. You should know that the full scholarship for law school, from the Gilchrest Foundation, that was me. Ryan, I already mentioned to Marcus that I was responsible for his vandalism charges being dropped. What I didn't mention is that you were also involved in those unsolved robberies, weren't you?"

Ryan slowly turned to Marcus, who only shrugged. Apparently, by the shocked looks on their siblings' faces, they hadn't shared their escapades.

"Owen, I'm sorry you had to step up and fill my shoes," Raymond continued. "And, Luke, I never expected you to follow in my footsteps. The military isn't a path I'd have chosen for any of you."

Then Alison was standing there with Brady, and he spotted Iris behind them, her hands resting on both their shoulders. Everyone turned.

"Okay, so, Owen, are you barbecuing?" Iris said. "Charlotte's hungry, Marcus, and says she wants something of substance, not crackers."

Owen said nothing for a second, just gave everything to Iris before dragging his gaze back to Raymond. "I have one question," he said. "If you're not Raymond O'Connell, and that name is on our birth certificates, who, exactly, does that make us, and who are you, really? I think we all want to know."

He could see this was the one question everyone shared. "It makes you Owen O'Connell, my son," he said. "I may not have existed until thirty-five years ago, but today, Raymond O'Connell does exist, on paper. I may have been put here, assigned here, and assumed an identity, but who I was before isn't who I am now. I've been Raymond O'Connell for thirty-five years." He stopped, but he could see they weren't going to let it drop, so he continued: "My name was David. I was born in Tel Aviv. I was pulled into Mossad as an informant when I was sixteen. I had gone sideways, mixing with the wrong crowd. I was a little shit, but I was quick at picking everything up, especially with people, learning everything that makes them laugh and smile, what bothers them. I could study and know people better than they knew themselves. It came naturally to me, and I was too good at it. I was the perfect recruit, and I was groomed well. I had a mother. Suzanne, you look like her."

His youngest touched her chest.

"She died when I was seventeen," he explained, "and so did David. I became Raymond O'Connell, and that's who I am. Brady, Baker was your mom's name. I assumed it for us to stay under the radar, but I'm afraid that's where we no longer are."

No one said anything. Jack was leaning against the wall, his arms crossed, and Harold was also standing off to the side, but he lifted his hand and said, "So let me understand this: Because you're here, everyone could be in danger."

He nodded.

Harold didn't pull his gaze. "Then what are you planning on doing?" he asked.

Raymond could see how unsettled everyone was. "Well, first, it seems this town has its sights set on screwing your mother around, as they've convicted her in the court of public opinion. They're basically waiting in the wings for all of you to do something wrong. So let's start with that Jolene Harris, who took your money, Iris, for the catering. We're getting it back. Marcus, schedule a press conference tomorrow with all the media, the DA, the mayor…"

Okay, now he had their attention.

"And why would I do that?" Marcus said, uncrossing his arms, with no surprise or alarm on his face. His son wasn't about to do his bidding or anything he asked.

He took in the shock on Iris's face and the way the kids

were trying to figure out what was going on. "Because it's time to go public, to set the record straight," Raymond said. "Staying in the shadows is no longer an option. I can't hide anymore. We also need to talk about some rules for everyone's safety. No one is alone, everyone checks in, and for now, Brady and I will be staying here."

He hadn't expected silence. Owen dragged his gaze over to Iris, who he could see was ready to kill him.

"And Alison, Brady..." He took a step and then hesitated, taking in his kids and then his granddaughter, who was staring at him in a way he wasn't sure what to make of. "All I can say is that I'm sorry."

Chapter Twelve

"I can't ask him to leave," Marcus said, the one thing Iris hadn't expected.

Owen strode past her to the fridge and gave the door a hard yank, then reached for a beer and twisted off the cap, which he tossed in the sink. He looked at her before dragging his gaze over to Marcus. Yeah, evidently, he was as unsettled as she was, but all he did was take a swallow and walk back outside, where Charlotte, Eva, Luke, Jenny, Ryan, and Harold were. Everyone else was in the living room with Raymond.

"Well, I don't understand why," Iris said and crossed her arms, feeling tension pull across her chest, the kind of tension she thought she had left behind long ago. "Last night shouldn't have happened. He shouldn't be here. I want him gone."

Marcus looked at her. "I know, Mom, but there's some stuff going on. Brady is so angry, and he doesn't want to leave. Do you want to toss him out, too?"

She let out a frustrated sigh. "No, I understand how Brady feels, and I'm sympathetic—but have you thought about Alison and how she's feeling? I sat outside with both of them, amid their teenage misery and silence. They couldn't even look at each other, let alone talk to each other. Maybe Brady should go…"

From the way Marcus leveled a glance at her, she could see he didn't agree. "I can take him to my place if that's what you want. I think you should know, though, that our father wants to do a press conference about the problems this town has caused for all of us, for you. You need to listen to what he's brought up. I never realized the problems that could exist for all of us. You know what? This isn't the time to toss anyone out. He's right about us all checking in."

She was aware of the way Marcus was avoiding using his dad's name, and she could see he was having trouble with it all. Her girls, her daughters, were still in the living room, and she was worried about how they were looking at Raymond.

"So now Raymond is suddenly in charge?" she said. "He tells you a story, a good one, and you're all suddenly falling into line?" She knew it had come out rather sharply, but she needed to get her son off the fence.

"Iris."

Speak of the devil! Raymond strode into the kitchen, and she didn't like the exchange between Marcus and him, as if to warn him she wasn't about to make anything easy.

"Yes, Raymond, what now? Oh, let me guess. You've just figured out another way to ruin my life."

Marcus stepped back and raised his brows. She was ready to fight and wasn't going to take anything lying down.

Raymond, though, didn't seem bothered in the least. "I want to talk to Alison and Brady together, to sit them down, because with everything going on, I think those two aren't going to take seriously how problematic things are right now. I thought you might want to weigh in and be there, considering…"

"Considering Brady wants nothing to do with you?" Iris said. "So what is this, good cop, bad cop? Are you trying to tell them how to think and feel? I can honestly tell you, from raising teens, there's nothing sweet about their personalities anymore. If you think they'll automatically fall in line, they won't. You seem to forget I raised six. I know how they think and the trouble they get into…"

"Not all the trouble," he cut in, and it felt like a slap. She pulled back, but he took another step closer. "Do you want to be there or not, Iris? I already talked to Ryan, and he thinks Alison hearing from me is a good idea."

For a second, she didn't know what to say, as it seemed her kids had suddenly turned traitor. "Fine, but watch yourself. Those kids are hurting, and that's entirely on you," she said. When she went to step around him, his hand gripped her arm, holding her right there. She knew he was looking at her, but she refused to look up. "Take your hands off me."

He leaned in closer, lowering his mouth to her ear. "Don't fight me, Iris," he said. "This isn't a game."

Then he stepped back, and Alison and Brady were behind him, standing in the doorway as if they'd been summoned. Iris was shaky, unsteady, but she'd be damned if she let this man hurt her, her children, her grandchildren again.

"Come on in here, you two," Raymond said.

Iris gestured to Alison, who was dressed rather conservatively in yoga pants and a T-shirt that wasn't unbelievably low cut. Even her normally heavy makeup was nonexistent today. She walked over to her grandmother, and Iris settled an arm over her shoulder, taking in an uncomfortable

Brady, who walked around his dad, way around him, to the island, and pulled out a stool to sit down.

"It's okay," Iris said to Alison, feeling how tense she was, knowing she'd probably cried her eyes out all night.

"Actually, it's not, Iris," Raymond cut in. His expression was pissed, irritated, and for a moment, she thought it was directed at her. "Brady, Alison, I need you two to really listen, because there are some ground rules that are going to apply to everyone, and that includes you two. I'm no longer in the shadows now. We're in the spotlight, and even though it's me who's responsible for this mess, this situation, it isn't me that my enemies will come after. They could come for any of you to get to me, to hurt me.

"So no one goes anywhere alone. No sneaking off. We check in. I've already talked to Luke and will sit down with everyone so we have a plan in place. I know you're both really angry with me, and rightly so. I've apologized to both of you and will continue to do so, because we, whether everyone likes it or not, are all family. Alison, you're my granddaughter, and I'm sorry this had to happen. Brady, you're my son, and I know you're furious, but every choice I made was for you. I couldn't be here, but you have to know everything I'm doing is to keep everyone safe. Right now, you probably both have a lot of questions, so let's put it all out there so we can figure this out."

Iris had to force herself not to look at Raymond, because even she wanted to believe him. She'd fight him all the way, though, if he thought she'd listen to him in any way or do what he wanted that easily. She understood the rebelliousness in her granddaughter more than anything now, because she couldn't deny that she too wanted to rebel against him.

"So you're my dad's dad," Alison said, crossing her

arms over her breasts, and Iris didn't miss the way Brady looked over to her.

"I am, Alison," Raymond said. "I'm your grandfather."

"Why the game?" she said. "I mean, I don't get this. The way you watched me, before, I didn't think you liked me."

Iris stared at Raymond, not too willing to step in and help him out even when he glanced over to her.

"It was never that I didn't like you, Alison," he said. "It was that I knew who you were and knew that you and Brady couldn't be more than friends."

"But you should have told the truth before, Dad," Brady said. "You shouldn't have lied. If you knew Alison was family, you should have sat me down and told me the truth, told me I had brothers and sisters. Instead, you just kept it a secret all these years, and now I'm supposed to just listen to you?"

She could see the edge in Raymond. Maybe he was having to remind himself that putting his hands on Brady wasn't the answer. She'd experienced that very same teenage angst from all her kids, each in a different way.

"Brady, I understand your anger better than anyone," Iris said. "In fact, your dad just being here has me fighting the urge to claw his eyes out—but I won't do that, because I'm civilized. Should Raymond have told you the truth?" She nodded, seeing the way Brady was listening to everything she was saying, and she gestured toward him, turning to Alison beside her, her other arm still around her. "Absolutely, without a doubt. He screwed up, big time, and not just with you, though you kids were the ones who suffered the biggest blow. I'd apologize, but I wasn't the one who lied. Yes, he should have told you. Yes, he should have come clean to all of us instead of sneaking around the way he was. I agree. But this is where we are. It's out. So right now, as a family…"

She stepped away from Alison, over to Brady, and reached for his hand, then held out her other to Alison, well aware that Raymond was watching everything. "We're going to figure this out together, okay? It doesn't mean you're giving your dad a pass, Brady." She let her meaning sink in and then dragged her gaze back over to Alison. "But staying safe is our number one priority right now." She squeezed both their hands gently when neither said anything. "Why don't you two go give Owen a hand outside?" She let them go and waited only a second, until Brady slipped off the stool, before sliding her hand around Alison's shoulders again.

Brady walked around Raymond without saying a word, then waited at the back door for Alison.

"Go with Brady," Iris said. "Come on. You're going to have to figure things out." She pressed a kiss to the side of Alison's head.

Alison shrugged and stepped away, following Brady out the door, and Iris gave everything back to Raymond, who was staring at her with a look she knew well. He had just realized she was the one with power over the kids, not him, and he wasn't happy about it.

"You know, it would help if you worked with me on this," he said.

"You mean if I just agreed with you, don't you?" she said, feeling as if she'd suddenly found her footing. "Yeah, well, you can get that idea out of your head." She slid her hand over the island and took a step closer to him, feeling more confident than she had in a long time.

He seemed unimpressed, and he didn't pull those eyes from her, those eyes that made her feel as though she were looking at her children.

"You see," she said, "I'm not the naïve young woman you married. Oh, wait—we're not really married."

His hand shot out so fast, gripping her wrist, that it startled her. His face said everything: She'd pushed too far. "Well, that's where you're wrong, Iris. As I told the kids in there, our kids, as far as the paperwork is concerned, I am Raymond O'Connell, and, that being so, you and I are still very much married."

Chapter Thirteen

The few leaves left on the trees had turned gold, but most of the branches were barren, ready for the first flakes of snow to fall. Even though the sun was out, Raymond could see his breath fog in front of him. He shoved his hands in the pockets of his dark fall jacket as he took in the handful of people on the steps in front of City Hall, the mayor and council members, all staring at him with the expressions he expected. They were unsmiling, pissed, just like his family, forced to be present for this stunt only because Luke and Jack had agreed with Raymond.

It seemed news had traveled, as he took in the mics and camera crews and reporters. The cameras flashed, capturing the missing Raymond O'Connell, who had stirred the rumor mill and had gossips' tongues wagging to shame the woman who was standing just behind the reporters, accompanied by Brady and both Karen and Suzanne.

Raymond allowed himself only a second to take in the faces watching him. "Good morning," he said. "I see you all found your way here. Just to clear the air of all the vicious rumors that have run through this town, I am Raymond O'Connell, and, as you can see, I'm very much alive and well. I'd like to say something to the people of Livingston, who've tried to hurt my wife and children with unsubstantiated lies. You all know who you are, because you're the ones who've hurt my wife badly at a time when she could have used your support.

"Yes, I said my wife. I'm still married to Iris, even though that's none of your business. Regardless, it seems this town has convicted her in the court of public opinion, saying she's guilty of something, and then there are the allegations about my children. Between the DA's office and all of you, I've watched from the sidelines as the family I abandoned eighteen years ago were railroaded. Let me be clear: I was the one who wronged them when I walked away. I'm confused as to how Iris could be accused of my murder when I'm alive and well. Is it really that easy to railroad an innocent person using an unidentified body?" He gestured and let the question hang. He had expected murmurs, but there was nothing.

"If you're not asking yourselves that very question, you should be, because that could have been you. How could this have happened to my wife? The current DA's office, under Tibo Lewis, twisted and manipulated evidence, claiming that the body of an unidentified man was mine. This is both alarming and disturbing, as the evidence was cleverly manipulated by the DA and some punk in the sheriff's office who tried to take my son's job. They were aware that the body in the woods couldn't have been mine, considering I had reached out and contacted them. To be clear, because of my lack of trust in this office and their handling of the matter, I also contacted the Feds to ensure that Deputy Lonnie and Tibo Lewis would not bury the details and continue to pursue an innocent woman, my wife, and my children, one of whom is the sheriff, Marcus O'Connell."

No one said anything, the cameras flashing. He knew everyone was hanging on his every word. Brady was still standing with Iris, too. At least he hadn't left, even if he still wasn't talking to him.

"Shame on you, all of you, in Livingston," Raymond said. "You know who you are, each and every one of you, who called Iris to make threats, to say angry words and spread lies about her. Just this week, someone took money to cater my son Ryan's wedding, then canceled on the day with no refund. Jolene Harris, you know what you did."

Marcus's lips twitched in a smile Raymond knew he was trying damned hard not to show.

"Iris never deserved that," he continued. "At the same time, an apology seems almost inadequate. Let's not forget the overreach in having Marcus removed as sheriff. That was merely payback, because he's the kind of sheriff, unlike most law enforcement officers in this country, who isn't afraid to take a stand. Marcus openly called out a district judge for his blatant bias, for his racism, and he refused to look the other way. That same Judge Root, in payback, signed a blanket search warrant for Iris's home, which was carelessly wrecked by several members of the current police force. It may seem coincidental that a sitting judge signed a blanket warrant that no judge with an understanding of civil rights would've signed, until you consider that Marcus, in his role as sheriff, was coming after that judge."

He paused again, hearing murmurs. The mayor's face was flushed, and for only a moment, he thought he caught a flash of humor in Marcus's expression again before it was gone.

"So, as you can see, I'm alive. The point of this press

conference is to set the record straight. Even though the charges had been dropped against Iris O'Connell, it was going to take my returning from the dead for you all to just stop, already. I need to ask each of you to keep one thing in mind. Ask yourself, if a DA can get a warrant without evidence and probable cause, could this happen to you too? An open warrant in any case is merely a fishing expedition, and that search resulted only in destruction at the hands of cops who had it out for my son. Personal items, memories, and photos were lost, not to mention the sheer invasion of privacy Iris underwent in having her home upended, with many things destroyed. What, exactly, did they uncover when they walked out with some of my belongings? They found a note I left, telling Iris, my wife, not to look for me. What the hell kind of evidence is that? To make it worse, they leaked the personal contents of that note and twisted the facts. That seems to be a pastime of the current DA, and I'm at a loss to understand how Tibo Lewis is still in office, elected, voted for by each of you." He gestured to the reporters.

"Mr. O'Connell, are you saying evidence was manufactured against your wife? If you left your family eighteen years ago, why did you leave? What happened to make you walk out? Did your wife do something?"

"Mr. O'Connell, what can you tell us about the reasons the DA went after your wife?"

The reporters were shouting over one another, and he wondered how many had actually heard a word he'd said. What spin would they put on this?

"What about the allegations that Sheriff O'Connell hid evidence? Did any of the O'Connells have any involvement in the murder, in the disposal of the body that was found?"

"Look…" He started laughing, taking in the faces of

the reporters. They wanted something, and the believ-ability of it was irrelevant—but he wasn't giving them everything they wanted. "I can tell you my family had no idea where I was. To be clear, this was a witch hunt, pure and simple. Why I left… Are you seriously asking that? You, down in front, young lady, did you seriously imply that my wife must have done something? I ran off, and she was somehow at fault?"

The young reporter's face flushed.

Raymond shook his head, taking in Iris, who was watching him in a way that he wasn't sure what to make of. "No, your questions are inappropriate," he said. "The truth of the matter is that I worked for the CIA for years. I'm ex-agency, and as Tibo Lewis and the federal govern-ment are aware, the body in the woods is that of a man who tried to come after my family to get to me. The man won't show up in any system, as his identity has been deemed a matter of national security. Know only that the deceased tried to get to me with plans to hurt my family."

"Mr. O'Connell, are you still with the CIA? Which organization tried to come after you?" one of the reporters called out.

He found himself looking over to Marcus, feeling the dangerous line he was walking.

"What about the remains, the body? Who was it?" shouted a different reporter, an older man in the back. "We were told he was a transient, with no ties to the area, but you're saying he wasn't."

"Look, first, you should know, 'transient man with no ties to the area' is just a phrase they use to shut down ques-tions when national security is involved. To answer your other question, I'm retired, which is why I'm here now. As far as which organization, I'm sorry, but I'm not at liberty to say, as the danger to my family is still very much an issue. That's one of the reasons I stayed away."

He listened to the barrage of questions, knowing what he'd just done, but if someone wanted to get to him or his family, at least he had made them more difficult targets.

Chapter Fourteen

"I don't understand something. Do the kids get together every night?" Raymond said.

Iris was standing outside Marcus's place after getting out of her Subaru, which Raymond had driven, though she still didn't know why she'd let him take her keys. She took in Ryan across the street, walking their way with Alison and Jenny. "We are close," she said. "Yes, many times during the week, we get together. We take turns on houses, mine, or Marcus's, or Ryan's. One of the kids brings beer, and Owen barbecues more times than not. Anything else?"

She didn't know why she felt defensive. Maybe she was still unsettled by what had happened at that news conference, which she still couldn't believe Marcus had arranged for him. Why was he going along with all of this for his dad? Raymond seemed less than forthcoming about everything, and maybe that was what bothered her more than anything. She knew he'd soon be gone again.

She wasn't sure what he was thinking as he strode around the Subaru and pocketed her keys. He filled out his dark jacket well in the cool fall air. Brady was riding with Karen, whose BMW she could see coming now.

As Ryan started over to her, she could see the open question on his face, likely about his dad, so she just lifted her hand and nodded as he called out, "Everything okay?"

"Yes, fine. We'll be right in," she said.

She wasn't sure what to make of the way Raymond was looking at Ryan, and vice versa, but then Alison, Jenny, and Ryan kept on walking into the house.

Raymond gave everything to her again. "Not something I expected, I guess. It's unusual. Families usually drift apart. They're not little kids anymore, and they have their own lives, but you all seem to center each other. I'm not saying it's a bad thing. I'm just saying it's unusual, is all." He stood right in front of her, and the way he looked down at her made her so uneasy.

"Well, we should go in, I guess…" she said, not knowing why she felt so damn nervous. Her hands were sweating where they were shoved in her jacket pockets.

"Look, I know I haven't handled any of this well, but you did a great job with the kids," he said. At the way he smiled, she could feel her anger coming out of nowhere again.

"Seriously?" she snapped. "I didn't have a choice, Raymond. I did the best I could, and just so you know, you get none of the credit. I had to hold them together. Don't think I've missed how Karen and Suzanne seemed to have given you a pass, but hear me: They're still in the honeymoon phase, full of nostalgia. Suddenly you're here, acting like some kind of hero, but you're not. I won't forget how you lied to me, Raymond."

He knit his brows. "I'm trying here, Iris…"

"What are you trying? You seem to forget that you

invaded my house after you created a lie and forced two kids to figure it out on their own, and you're still in my house, and now it seems you have no intention of leaving." She held up the flat of her hand when he went to cut in. "No, Raymond, let me finish. This is turning into something that isn't right. Yes, thank you for that public show today, but I guarantee you it will resolve squat, because the O'Connells are once again in the spotlight, front and center. You won't be staked publicly and humiliated the way the kids and I were, maybe because you're a man, and people give men a pass, especially when they look like you—"

"Iris," Jack called out from behind her, and she turned her head sharply. She hadn't realized anyone was there or how loud she was. Her heart raced, and she had to pull in a breath.

Brady was standing with Karen at her BMW, staring at her in a way that made her wish she could go back in time by two minutes and shut her damn mouth.

Jack was walking toward her, bearing down on her, and then he was there. "I want to talk to you," he said, then turned to Raymond. "Could you give us a minute?"

"Of course," Raymond said, though Iris knew Jack wouldn't have given him a choice. He glanced only a second at Iris before resting his hand on her shoulder and then walking around her. It was intimate and personal, and she knew Jack had picked up on all of it.

"Sorry, I'm just…" she started.

He settled his gaze on her, his icy blue eyes so different from Raymond's. "Don't apologize, seriously," he said. "I wanted to check in and touch base. Do you know what you're getting yourself into, having Raymond in your life, in your house?"

Karen and Brady were walking to the house, giving her

and Jack space. Evidently, her daughter knew this talk was not to be interrupted.

"It's not as if I had a choice here, Jack. I didn't want him in my house, but he insisted because he won't leave without Brady. He's playing the overprotective papa, is all. He'll be gone sooner rather than later, I assume." She lifted her hands.

Her son-in-law, who'd basically saved all of them just days earlier, didn't pull his gaze from her. "You know, Iris, he may have planned on leaving, but I can tell you, from where I'm standing, I doubt that's on the table now. He basically put a spotlight on where he is, and that news conference today will have his people realizing that touching him now would raise questions no one wants. He's still a hunted man, Iris, and him being here puts a target on everyone, but I think you know that. I know Karen doesn't want to hear it because she's stuck on the idea of her dad being back. I can see how much she wants some type of fairy tale with you and Raymond being together, or at least her dad being back for good. She doesn't want to see the danger he brings, even though she stood there at that news conference and heard everything. He may have been the one to see to it that those charges against you were dropped, but I want to be sure you're not seeing the situation for anything other than it is."

This wasn't what she'd expected from Jack. "I can assure you I'm no longer starry eyed, and I don't believe in fairy tales, considering mine turned into a nightmare," she said. "It's only a matter of time before he leaves, Jack. His priority is Brady. I see that. I don't want any of my children thinking that Raymond came back and is here for them. Karen was his favorite, even though he loved all of them. When he left, she took it hardest, and I got the brunt of it, because she's a mini me. That's

Raymond's quote, but he's right. Out of all my kids, Karen is most like me in so many ways. I hear you loud and clear, everything you're saying." She let out a sigh and wasn't sure what to make of the way Jack was watching her. Then he reached over and rubbed her shoulder.

"You know, you're wrong about one thing. Raymond may be here for Brady, but everything he's doing and has done has been for you, for all of you. Now, by no means am I in his corner or happy he's here. I just want to be sure you're seeing everything clearly, is all, because the direction this is headed could end up with you and Karen being hurt —or all of you. Me, I have no emotional attachment to the man, but I see each of you is terrified of being hurt, and you're angry, and, even though I doubt any of you will admit you want something more, there's also a flicker of hope. I wonder if any of you have any idea it's there or that you secretly want something you know you can't have. You know the kind of danger I'm talking about, as your lawyer. No one else saw that letter. I'm well aware of the mother's fear you operated under to protect your children."

Why was it that talking to Jack only added to what she already knew?

"I'm under no illusion that a happily ever after could happen here," she said. "But what about Brady? Raymond won't leave without his son. I've asked him to go, but…"

Jack dragged his gaze up to the house. "You know, Brady can come and stay with one of us. Then Raymond will have no reason to stay, if that's what you're looking for."

She pulled in a breath, seeing Luke's old pickup approaching from down the street. "Yeah, we should go in," she said instead of answering, aware that it was an option. Then Raymond would be gone, and that was something she didn't want to think of right now.

Jack nodded, then shook his head. "Fine, but think about what I said. Ask yourself what you really want out of this."

Then he started to the house, and she took in Luke, who pulled up and parked. Voices drifted out from Marcus's house behind her, and she pulled in another breath, feeling that constant unsettled feeling that just didn't want to go away.

Chapter Fifteen

WHAT WAS IT ABOUT JACK? RAYMOND COULDN'T SHAKE the feeling that the man could be a problem for him, especially considering that after his talk outside with Iris, she'd done everything she could to avoid him. She wouldn't even look his way where he stood in the kitchen of Marcus's house, where food filled the counter. Little Eva, Marcus and Charlotte's adopted daughter, was sitting on a stool, staring at him, holding a glass of juice.

"Eva, if you're done, why don't you go and find your cousin?" Charlotte said from where she was rinsing lettuce at the sink.

He'd expected her to say something to him. Instead, Eva just put the glass down and slid off that stool, then started out of the kitchen. But she stopped and looked back at him.

"I don't think she knows what to say to you. She's curious, is all," Charlotte said.

He hadn't realized she was watching him. He stood by the island, holding a beer Marcus had handed him before joining the others in the living room. Owen and Tessa were out back, with their coats on, by the smoking barbecue.

"Does Owen always barbecue?" Raymond said. It was cold out, but he could see them from the window. Owen had gone out of his way to avoid him.

Charlotte moved away from the sink and started ripping the clean lettuce into a bowl on the island. She lifted her hand and pressed it into her lower back. He could see she was uncomfortable.

"Why don't you sit down here?" he said. "Come on. I'll do the lettuce."

"You sure?" she said.

He put down his beer and pulled the stool out, then gestured to it, and Charlotte walked around and slid onto it. He picked up the lettuce and started ripping it up, not missing the way she groaned. He didn't know why, but it made him remember Iris and how many nights he had rubbed her swollen feet and ankles while she carried his children.

"Owen is kind of the head of the family," Charlotte said. "He looked after all the kids. As long as Marcus and I have been together, this has been what Owen does. You should try talking to him. He's overprotective of everyone because he's had to be, but he's steady."

Charlotte glanced out to him. Owen had the lid up on the barbecue and was turning the chicken he'd insisted on cooking. He wondered if he'd ever figure out a way to reach his son. Anger was anger, and Owen had stepped into his role overnight. He could feel how much he disliked him. He noticed that Charlotte was staring over to him as if trying to figure him out.

"You know, I remember how tired Iris got with all the kids running around," he said. "By the time she was pregnant with Suzanne, she had Owen helping with Ryan and

Marcus. Luke had always been the difficult one, getting into everything. Marcus…he was damn smart, and he got into trouble I don't think his mom still has any idea about. You could see him thinking, planning, doing… Then there was Ryan, who followed everything Marcus did."

A smile touched her lips. "Well, maybe that's why Marcus is the best at what he does, the best sheriff this town has ever had. He knows where to look when someone has committed a crime. No one else knows where to start, but he just does. Then again, I'm rather partial to him."

The way she talked about his son had him smiling. Just then, he spotted Karen walking his way, wearing a fuchsia dress with a light sweater and heels. Her hair was a mix of blond and red, and she reminded him of Iris at her age. She looked so much like her mom.

"Hi, Dad. What are you two talking about?" she said as she slid on a stool next to Charlotte.

"You know what? I'm going to leave you two and go put my feet up in the living room," Charlotte said, running her hand over Karen's arm before slipping off the stool and walking out.

Raymond finished ripping the lettuce. He could see how close they all were.

"I hope I didn't interrupt?" Karen said, and he could feel her hesitation.

"Darlin', you're never interrupting. So tell me about you, everything about you and that husband of yours, who seems to have his eye on me." He rested his hands on the island and took in the smile that touched Karen's lips as she glanced out to the living room, where he knew Jack was with everyone else.

"Jack is just Jack. He wants to make sure none of us gets hurt, is all. Dad, can I ask you something?" She flicked her blue eyes up to him the way she'd done as a little girl, when he'd have done anything for her.

"Hey, you can ask me anything. What is it? That husband of yours, you need me to talk to him for you? He'd better be treating you right."

That brought a teasing smile to her face, but she shook her head. "No, it's something Jack said, but he's right. I need to know if you're going to be here tomorrow or if you're going to disappear again."

He spotted Suzanne walking hesitantly their way, and he stood from where he was leaning. "Hey, come on in here," he said. "I haven't had a chance to talk to you, either."

Suzanne was a tomboy, always had been, tall and slim. If his mother were there, he wondered what she'd think of Suzanne. It was her face; she looked just like his mom, bringing up all the nostalgia he'd never expected to feel again.

"Well, I came to grab another beer for Harold…" she started.

He knew Karen was still waiting for his answer. "Your sister just asked if I'm planning on taking off again," he said.

Suzanne moved beside Karen and didn't pull her blue eyes from him. He could tell she was evidently thinking the very same thing.

"I guess you all deserve an answer. I left you so many years ago, and it wasn't by choice. At the same time, I didn't plan on still being here. I love you all so very much, you girls and your brothers, and…"

And Iris, he thought, but he stopped himself from saying it, because he could see something in their eyes that he couldn't encourage. It was the kind of hope he knew would crush his girls.

"But I never stopped watching you, doing what I could from a distance," he said.

They were so quiet, saying nothing, waiting for him to say…what, that he'd stay forever? He couldn't do that.

"I never knew," Suzanne said. "I don't understand, though. Why couldn't you reach out?"

She had no idea, he realized. He could see now that she still didn't get it.

"Anyone seen Brady and Alison?" Ryan said as he strode into the kitchen, holding Eva's hand.

Raymond could see that Suzanne and Karen were still waiting for him to give them the one thing they wanted. "No, I thought they were in the living room," he started.

Suzanne shook her head. "No, I saw them go upstairs with the remotes and video player."

"They're not there," Ryan said. "The video player was just sitting in the spare room by the TV, not hooked up. They didn't come back down? Eva is looking for them, and I don't remember the last time I saw them. They're not out back, are they?"

"I've been in the kitchen the entire time," Raymond said. "They'd have had to walk past me…"

The back door opened, and Owen strode in with Tessa, her cheeks pink from the cold. He could smell the chicken that filled the platter Owen carried.

"What's going on?" Owen asked without looking at him.

"We can't find Alison and Brady," Raymond said. "You didn't see them?"

That forced Owen to look over to him. "Nope, I haven't. Just me and Tessa out back. Check the front porch?"

Marcus walked in then, wearing a blue and white T-shirt and blue jeans. His dark hair looked as if he'd run his hands through it. "What's going on here? You find the kids?" He looked at each of them.

Raymond didn't know why, but the warning he'd given all of them was echoing in his mind. Stay together, check in. Those damn kids were trying to sneak off and do the opposite!

"They're not upstairs or out back. Are they out front?" Raymond said. He went to take a step around the island, around Owen.

Marcus dragged his gaze from the front door to him. "No, they're not," he said. Then he had his cell phone to his ear, and he shook his head. "Alison's not answering. It went to voicemail. I don't hear it ringing in the house." He dialed again. "I'll try Brady."

They all waited.

Marcus shook his head. "Nope, voicemail. Ryan, maybe they snuck over to your place."

Suzanne stood, and Ryan lifted Eva and sat her on the empty stool beside Karen, whose arm went instantly around her.

"I'll go check," Ryan said.

"I'll go with you," Raymond said, following, but he stopped in front of Marcus. "I don't want to sound the alarm bells, but…"

Marcus shook his head. "I get it. Go and look. I'm sure they're over at Ryan's, and then we'll sit them down and have a talk with them again so they understand there's no more bullshit and sneaking off."

He just had a bad feeling, though, as he followed Ryan to the door. Iris, who was holding a glass of wine, was walking his way along with Jenny, Ryan's pretty wife. The front door was open, and Luke and Harold were already outside. He rested his hand on his son's shoulder before they started out.

"You know Brady is angry, but I can't understand him taking off like this," Raymond said. "This isn't like him. Even as angry as he is, he's not like this."

"Well, Alison is a different story," Ryan said. "This is something she's done. For all we know, they just wanted a little space, but I swear, when I get my hands on her…" Ryan didn't finish.

Raymond took in the concern in Iris's expression, but he pulled his gaze away, following Ryan out of the house. They just stood on the front porch, taking in the neighborhood, the cars on the street. With this middle-class suburbia came a warning, a feeling that something wasn't right. Raymond just hoped that this time, his instincts were wrong.

Chapter Sixteen
<hr>

There was no sign of the kids.

Anywhere.

Ryan and Jenny were furious, and Charlotte was sitting with little Eva on the sofa. Iris could see how the worry was taking its toll.

"The back door at Ryan and Jenny's was open, and the lock was splintered. I found this." Raymond held up the hoodie Brady had been wearing. "It was on the floor at the back door. How did they even get out of the house without anyone seeing?" The way he said it sounded so accusatory.

Marcus paced at the foot of the stairs, his cell phone to his ear, talking to one of his deputies, she thought, or maybe it was someone else. Harold pulled open the screen door, which squeaked. He had already pulled on his deputy's jacket, and he handed something to Marcus and said something to him. Marcus was listening to whoever he was talking to on the other end, then nodded. They really did have a good working relationship.

"Do you think the kids took off, or is it that Raymond being here brought a world of trouble down on us?" Owen said, still wearing his dark all-season coat. She knew he'd been outside, over at Ryan's. Tessa was now sitting on the sofa on Eva's other side. Iris took in her eldest, who'd been there for all of them. He wasn't giving an inch, still seeing Raymond as the enemy.

"Well, Alison has a way about her," Iris said. "You know that. Being reasonable and making things easier for everyone are things she doesn't do well. But taking off… Let's hope it's just as simple as the kids slipping out together deliberately to worry all of us. At the same time, Owen, ease up on your dad."

Owen hesitated before dragging his gaze back over to her. From his expression, he seemed to really dig in. "And when did you jump to Raymond's side?"

She rested her hand on his arm. "Don't look at me like that, and don't be so obstinate, either. This isn't about sides, Owen. This is about keeping everyone safe. You can still be angry. Everyone has a right to be, and you especially, but you have to be able to set it aside so we can find Brady and Alison. At the same time, I'm not completely blameless here, considering I'm the one who created this mess for you kids…"

"No, Mom, you're not," he said. "You were scared, but he ran out. You did what a mother's supposed to do to protect her kids. What did he do?"

She could see his point of view, how one sided it was, filled with so much resentment. "Okay, I get it, but let's table this for now. How about we all work together, find the kids, and then we can talk about this more? I think, for your sake, you need to talk to him. This isn't about me; this is about you two. You don't have to like him, Owen, and you can still be angry, but you have a way of holding things in, and I know I'm responsible for that." She ran her hand over his arm again, over his shoulder.

Ryan was already walking out the door, and she knew that Jenny, Luke, and Jack were across the street. She could see the lights on.

"I'm going to go over," Owen said. "Tessa, stay here with Charlotte and my mom." He seemed to hesitate for a second. "Okay, I take your point, but consider it tabled for now." He rested his hand on her shoulder as well, then pulled it away.

She realized Raymond was staring at her from where he stood with Marcus and Harold. Owen was gone, and Raymond watched him as he walked out the door, then glanced back to her. She started over to him, hearing Suzanne and Karen in the kitchen.

"So what's the verdict here?" Iris said. "Where do we start? It's now pitch dark outside. Any ideas? Come on, I'm sure one of you has something. Let's be honest here. This is completely up Alison's alley, sneaking out with Brady…"

All three were looking at each other, and she had the feeling they knew more.

"No, that wouldn't explain the busted lock on the back door at Ryan and Jenny's," Marcus said. "We were over here, all of us, and no one was there. How did they get out of the house? I didn't see them slip out, but then, we didn't exactly have a guard posted at the door." He looked down at her, and she knew he wasn't holding anything back.

Harold hesitated before saying, "Luke has called someone he works with to get into the kids' phones."

"Sienna and her team," Raymond cut in. "She's CIA. She trained under Brady's mother."

For a second, Iris was speechless.

"I'm going to head back over to Ryan's after I talk to Suzanne," Harold said, then slipped away to the kitchen behind her. Then Marcus did as well, and that left her and

Raymond and the awkwardness of what was beginning to seem like too small of a world.

Raymond rested his arm on the bannister of the stairs, and for a moment the silence lingered between them.

"So, this Sienna, who works with Luke, was aware of you?" Iris said. "She said nothing to Luke, obviously, because I know he's been looking for you for years. I suspected it but only found out recently."

Raymond looked past her, and she wondered what he wasn't going to say. "She knew, but in the CIA, secrets are your life. Luke knows that. He signed on for the same thing, just like I did. It's the life we picked. Luke is aware now. But this is about finding the kids, getting them back here. I didn't expect this, but maybe I should have. I got too comfortable, Iris. I made that mistake once before, and you know what happened."

She could feel the end coming again. "So you're saying the government you work for—"

"Worked for, past tense. I left them. I told you that, but I didn't tell you everything. I have an insurance policy, copies of the kind of dirt every country has but would never want in the wrong hands. It's just that my threat doesn't seem to be effective."

She heard footsteps outside just as the screen door was yanked open.

"Dad," Luke called. It was the first time she'd heard any of her kids call him that since he'd been back. Luke gestured to him, holding the door open, and Raymond walked out. Instead of staying put, Iris followed, taking in the surprise on their faces.

"Whatever you have, Luke, this isn't the time for secrets," she said. "We've gone way past that. I may not understand how all these government agencies work, or the politics, or who these people are, or why they want to hurt us, but I'm well aware of the kind of evil that's out there. I've seen enough, so whatever it is…" She gestured to them all.

Luke seemed to hesitate before lifting his gaze over to his dad. She could see some type of connection, one she wasn't sure she was that happy to see. "My team is working it," he said. "They found something on Alison's phone, a text from an unknown blocked number that said if they wanted to know the truth, the real truth, about Brady, they needed to find a way to sneak out of the house and go over to Ryan's. Evidently, someone was in the house, waiting for them. All we can assume at this point is that whoever it was took them."

Her arms were crossed over her chest, and even though it was cold out, the chill she felt had nothing to do with that. "And what now? How do we find them?" she said, catching another unreadable exchange between Luke and his father.

"We already found them," Luke said. Raymond seemed to know what that meant, by the way he glanced away, looking out into the darkness.

"And? Come on, you two, out with it," she said. "What does this mean? If you found them, go get them. Or am I missing something here?"

Maybe it was that second of hesitation that seemed to ramp up the uneasiness that had found a way to wedge itself deeper into the pit of her stomach.

"They want me, don't they?" Raymond said, not looking her way.

Luke didn't nod, but he did take a second to look down at Iris. "Yeah," he said. "They called Jenny and texted a photo of Alison and Brady to her cell phone. They want you, and then they'll let the kids go."

Raymond said nothing. He seemed to be thinking,

considering. That was just something about him, she realized, that she'd never really understood.

"If they don't get Raymond, then what?" she said. "Did they give a time frame or anything else?"

Raymond gestured to Luke and then turned, looking down at her. Just his one look made her think she'd be sick because of how tight the knot was getting. He sighed. "If I don't go and hand myself over, give them what they want, the kids will be dead. It's not an option."

This was worse than she could have imagined. She stared at the man who was the love of her life, the man who had broken her heart by leaving, then by coming back. She had known it couldn't last, but now, as she stared at him, she realized she wasn't ready to say goodbye again. Maybe that was why she looked over to Luke when she said, "And there's no other way?"

Her voice had cracked. She felt Raymond's hand on her shoulder.

Luke nodded to the house. "I'm going to get Marcus and Harold up to speed," he said, then pulled open the door, leaving Raymond and Iris alone outside.

"Look, we knew this was going to happen at some point," he said. "There's no choice, Iris. This is the kids. Damn them for taking off! Still, it was just a matter of time. This is the only way to make sure they don't come after anyone else." He had both his hands on her shoulders and was standing so close that the ache in her chest seemed too much.

"There has to be another way…" she said, but he was already shaking his head.

"Them getting their hands on one of you was the thing I feared, and now they have. Iris, when I left you, there was so much left unsaid. This time, I need you to know that the happiest time of my life was with you. After all those years with you, walking away was the hardest thing I had to do. They say everyone has that one great love in life. Well, for me, that was you." He rubbed her shoulders, his hands sliding up over her cheeks. He was so close, and she could see it there in his eyes, how hard this was.

"Damn you to hell, Raymond O'Connell! You're going to do it to me again, aren't you?" she said. Her eyes blurred, and she could feel the kind of tears she hadn't cried in years coming out of nowhere.

He pulled her close in his arms and just held her as she tried to fight a losing battle against the despair that just wouldn't stay away.

He pressed a kiss to the top of her head and murmured softly, "I never for one moment stopped loving you, Iris. Just know that. I love you."

But as she fisted her hands in his shirt, feeling his arms holding her, she wished for a moment that he could be anyone but who he really was.

Chapter Seventeen

HE TOOK IN MARCUS, RYAN, AND LUKE, WHO WAS DRIVING Ryan's pickup, as they parked around the back of the house he'd rented. They had swung by Iris's home, the house he'd bought for their growing family, where Luke had grabbed the black bag full of guns, ammo, and gear that Luke kept hidden beneath a floorboard under his bed. Even he hadn't known it was there.

He was in the back seat, beside Ryan, and he took in the darkened neighborhood, the back alley, the fact that he didn't know for sure who would be waiting for him. "If anything goes wrong, I want your word you'll look after Brady," he said.

Marcus glanced back to him. "He's family. It goes without saying. You ready?"

Luke pulled the keys from the ignition and opened the door to step out. He had on a black knit hat and seemed to blend into the darkness. Ryan said nothing, but Raymond could hear him checking his gun as he closed his door.

He blew out a breath, still picturing the image that had been texted to Jenny's phone: Brady and Alison with duct tape over their mouths, hands and feet tied, sitting back to back on the old carpet in front of the fireplace. The tears on Alison's face and her terrified expression had gotten to him. It was that emotional attachment that would be his downfall.

These brilliant assholes would keep going after his Achilles' heel, his family. They'd just never stop.

"Let's go before time's up," he said.

Luke only nodded as he started walking with him around front.

"You think Marcus and Ryan will keep their heads together?" Raymond said.

"They'll get the kids out. Just worry about what you need to do, and that's it. You start focusing on everyone else, and that's when everything goes sideways. Jack and Owen will make sure everyone back home stays put and safe. We know how to pull together."

He took in the darkened house and wondered where they'd be when he walked in. As he took in the vehicles on the street, he didn't see one that looked out of place.

"There's a lot I wanted to say to each of you, but there's no time," he said, "so I'm going to say this: You have a chance at love, Luke. Take it. That girl you've been sneaking around with, Rosemary, you have your reasons for keeping her a secret, but don't."

He could feel Luke glance to him and then back to the house. "So you know about her. Of course you do. It's not that easy."

"It is that easy. The only reason you think it isn't is because you keep telling yourself so."

Luke didn't answer him.

His heart kicked up. They were halfway across the front grass, and he kept walking to the darkened front door. He put his hand on the knob, taking a look back to Luke, who was pressed with his back to the side of the house not far from him. His son gestured for him to open the door.

He wished he had more time. He wished he could have said something more to each of them, especially Owen, whom he'd pulled aside before leaving. He'd told his son how proud he was of him and that he loved him. Owen had said nothing, but then, he hadn't waited for him to say anything. He remembered the confusion that had knit his brows.

Then there was Iris. It seemed the years they'd had together were all they were going to get.

He turned the knob, seeing every one of his kids' faces, little, grown, and then the face of his wife.

He stepped inside the house, leaving the front door open. "I'm here," he called out, "so let the kids go."

From the front entryway, he could see the steps that went up to the living room and the darkness of the rest of the house. He lifted his hands in the air. The kids were by the fireplace, and he could hear their muffled voices just before he felt hard steel against the back of his head.

"You have me now," he said. "Let the kids go."

A hand lifted his jacket and ran over him, looking for a gun, reaching for the one he had tucked at the small of his back. "Step up and call your son in," the man said. "Come on inside, Luke. Put your gun down."

He didn't recognize the deep male voice. He didn't have to look over to see that Luke was in the doorway, and as he took a step up into the living room, he felt weakness settle into his legs. The effort it took for him to step up was huge. He saw another shadow, then someone else lingering in the doorway of the kitchen. He knew the man was holding a gun, but he couldn't see his face in the darkness.

The man behind him put a hand on his shoulder, kicked his leg out from under him, and pushed him to his knees. His hands were pulled behind his back and zip-tied, and he could feel the plastic dig into his wrists.

"Get down, you motherfucker." The voice was raspy. "You betray your government, your people, you'll be dragged back to face treason charges and be made an example of."

He wished he could see his face. He heard the sound of his gun being emptied of bullets and tossed behind him on the ground.

"You have your trade, Raymond for Brady and Alison," Luke called out. "Let the kids go."

"First, where's the list, Raymond?" asked the man.

How many were there? Three for sure. They wanted everything that could embarrass and expose his country, all its dirty secrets. But the minute they had it, no one would be walking out of there. He knew well that if any of what he had came to light, it would embarrass his country in a way they wouldn't stand for: the two sitting judges who had been placed under surveillance, the presidential hopeful who had lost his nomination, the classified economic and political analysis that had been obtained for clients of a security firm that represented only the top one percent, the assassinations of scientists working in arms manufacturing…and that wasn't even everything.

"That wasn't the deal," Raymond said. "The deal was me for the kids. Let them go, and then I'll tell you where the copies are, where everything is, everything that could embarrass the prime minister. I kept everything in case a day like this happened, and I'm sure you've done the same. Although valuable, you're also a liability, because you know that if any of what you've done comes to light, it would embarrass the country—and no one wants that. No one will stand for that. So, again, only after the kids are safe will you get anything. You got me. That's who you wanted. Now let them go."

Then a light flicked on in the dining room, and he realized there were four. He took in a man he hadn't seen in years. Saul Gusterson was older now, but he was still tall, and he still had that look, as if he knew everything was about to go sideways.

Saul walked over to the kids, the gun in his hand, the silencer screwed on. He held it up and over them, gesturing with his gun to one, then the other. Alison was staring in horror, trembling, and Brady was looking to him to do something.

"Pick one," Saul said. It was there in the sound of his voice, the killer in him. He wouldn't hesitate. He knew what it took to pull the trigger.

Raymond yanked at his arms, feeling the bite of the plastic, but the welcome pain did nothing to free him. "No, stop! I'll tell you where it is!" he yelled.

Just then, he felt pain explode across his chest, and everything happened in slow motion. There was the sound of glass shattering, then screams and shouts. Another shot was fired, and he was face down on the carpet now, wetness pooling across his chest.

He could hear the chaos vaguely, the screams, the yelling. But all he could see was his wife, her smile, and the way she had looked at him so long ago.

Then there was nothing else.

Chapter Eighteen

IRIS COULDN'T REMEMBER THE LAST TIME SHE HAD WORN black.

She stood in the most uncomfortable heels in the cold as the snow started to fall. The cemetery was empty except for the small group around the fresh grave. Her children, her family, were standing with her, along with a minister she didn't recognize, who was talking about a man he didn't know.

Raymond was the love of her life.

He'd broken her heart, then come back only to open the wound that hadn't healed, and then he'd left her again. Now, the words being spoken for a man she'd cried for eighteen years earlier didn't seem to touch on who he really was.

He was a secret. He was theirs. These were his children.

Raymond O'Connell hadn't been who he said he was, but now she knew he really had loved her and the kids. He'd held her and kissed her, then walked away with his sons, and it seemed as if everything in her world had come full circle. She was having to remind herself again and again that he'd put himself between danger and his family.

She took in the coffin being lowered into the ground, then Brady, who was standing between Karen and Suzanne, their arms around him, even though he was taller than them. His youth really came through in the hollowness and sorrow of his face. She needed to talk to him, but she couldn't, not after hearing the way he'd broken down.

"Mom, you okay?" Marcus said. He was holding Eva's hand, and Charlotte's, and they were looking at her as if they thought she was fragile and broken.

But Iris was stronger than that. She'd had to be. Instead of saying anything as Marcus waited, she found herself seeing how much of his dad was in him, from the way he walked, to his expression. Even the way he eventually looked away was so much like Raymond. She had to turn from him, shrugging, unable to find a reasonable thing to say.

Early winter was upon them.

"It's cold out here," she finally said. "You should take Charlotte and Eva to the car."

Then she walked around Marcus and over to the grave, where she picked up a handful of dirt, even though the ground was starting to freeze. As the casket was lowered, she tossed the dirt on top.

She took in the hollow expression on Alison's face. She was sandwiched between Ryan and Jenny, holding their hands. There were cuts on her forehead from where the glass had hit her. She leaned against Ryan, who put his arm around her and pulled her closer, kissing the top of her head.

She hadn't taken any time to talk to her teenage misfit or to anyone at all. For reasons she couldn't explain, the loss of Raymond was so much worse than anything she could bear. Maybe it was because this time, she knew it was permanent. He was gone forever and was never coming back.

Jack had taken her arm and was leading her to his car. Karen was behind them with Brady, and Harold and Suzanne were following, as were Owen and Tessa.

"You don't have to walk me, Jack. You should go look after your wife," she said, though she didn't have to look over to him to know that he wasn't about to listen.

"You know Karen is worried about you," he said. "We all are. And yeah, I do need to walk you. That's what family does."

She slipped into the backseat after he held the door open, and then Luke was there in the doorway. He pulled something from his jacket and pressed it into her hand—an airline ticket.

"What's this?" She took in the ticket and how Luke's blue eyes, his dad's eyes, took her in.

"It's a plane ticket," he said. "You need to take some time for yourself right now. It was the last thing Dad gave me. He told me to give it to you. He had rented a place on the beach in Barbados, paid for it and everything. He was planning on taking Brady there. Then this…"

She just stared at the ticket, feeling the ache that wouldn't go away, which pulled at her chest. The tears that burned her eyes threatened to fall again. Jack was standing in front of the car with Karen and Brady as if he knew what was happening, and the last thing she wanted to do was cry anymore in front of her kids, so she bit her lip hard, taking another second to will herself to pull it together.

She was stronger than this. She had to be there for her kids, her family. She clutched the ticket and felt Luke's hand over hers. He squatted down and glanced to the side. She wondered how uncomfortable he was.

"Go, Mom," he said. "The flight leaves tonight. Dad wanted you to have this. You deserve it. Spend a few weeks on the white sandy beach, drink a beer or a margarita, read a book, put your feet in the warm baby blue of the ocean, and just take time for yourself. Do it for Dad."

She had to press her hands over her face, as she couldn't hold back the tears that fell. She felt Luke's hand on her back, and he said, "It's okay. It's going to be okay."

He just let her cry for a minute. When she pulled her hand away, taking in the ticket he'd given her, she could feel how different this ending was.

"This isn't fair," she said, finally finding the words for something she didn't know how to say.

Luke glanced away again and pressed his hand to her leg, then held the door, saying nothing. He closed it just as Brady climbed into the back with her, and Karen and Jack got in front.

She tucked the ticket in her pocket and turned to the gravesite they had just walked away from. It was so final. She reached over to the young man who sat quietly beside her and squeezed his hand, then patted it, but she didn't say it was going to be okay. Instead, she said nothing.

Jack started the car and pulled away, and she wondered this time how long it would take for the overwhelming sorrow, which had stolen all her energy, happiness, and joy once before, to fade. Would she be able to put her feet on the floor in the morning and get out of bed again instead of wanting to crawl back in and pull the covers up over her head?

It had taken days, weeks, months before. She told herself it should be better this time, but for a reason that didn't make sense to her, it now seemed far worse.

Suzanne and Jenny had packed her suitcase, and Marcus had tossed it in the back of her car, which Luke had driven to take her to the airport even though she hadn't wanted to go. None of them would hear her arguments. Now here she was, in a country she'd never been to before, alone, when the best thing for her would've been to be with her family.

The heat was welcome, the sun was bright, and the humidity soaked her white T-shirt as she took in the cottage on the ocean. It was white and cute.

The man who'd driven her smiled, his teeth bright white against his dark skin. "Mrs. O'Connell, this is it. You call me and let me know if you need anything," he said as he walked back from the cottage after carrying her two large suitcases in for her.

Her purse was over her shoulder, and she realized this was where she was supposed to tip him, so reached into it, but he just shook his head.

"No, no, no," he said. "It's all taken care of. Your suitcases are on the front porch, and here are the keys. Can I get you anything else?"

She took the set of keys from him. The breeze had kicked up, though it did little to help with the heat. She felt the way her shirt stuck to her back. Even the light cotton slacks she'd traveled in felt too heavy in this heat, and she was so tired from the hours on the plane that she wanted a shower and maybe a nap. She took in the man, who was still waiting for an answer, and shook her head. The place was private, but she knew it wasn't that far of a walk to the shops and restaurants.

"No, that's fine, thank you," she said, then watched as he lifted his hand and walked back to the old jeep, in which he'd picked her up at the airport and driven her across the island to this spot, which she had to admit was beautiful.

Her sunglasses on, she started to the house. On the porch, she took in her bags and the way the waves crashed against the shore. She breathed in the salty air, the warmth, and then turned to the door and slid the key in the lock.

Inside the cottage, a towel was tossed over the orange and brown sofa, and two glasses were sitting on the counter with a gift basket of wine. Evidently, they had figured she'd be with someone. She reached for the bottle of red, knowing Karen would've loved it.

"You sure you want a glass this early?"

She damn near dropped the bottle. She felt the floor beneath her soften, hearing a voice she'd thought she'd never hear again, and she turned around.

Emotion hit her hard, right in the stomach, so hard that for a second, she had to remind herself to breathe. He was barefoot in shorts and a white T-shirt, and he lifted his sunglasses and stepped into the cottage—tall, dark, handsome, and not dead.

"What is this?" Her voice sounded off. Her heart was pounding as he stepped closer.

"You look as if you've seen a ghost," he said, walking right over to her.

When she pressed her hands to her face, she couldn't stop the tears. "Damn you, Raymond O'Connell! What...? How...?"

That was all she could get out, as he was right there in front of her, his arms around her, and he had pulled her tight against him. He kissed the top of her head as she cried against him, and he held her so tight until she could stop this damn crying.

She slid her hands over his chest, looking up at him, a man she loved so deeply.

"It was the only way to be truly free," he said. "So you and the kids wouldn't be hunted forever, I had to die."

She pulled her hand across her face again and took him in. "I don't understand. Did the kids know? How? I was told you were killed, shot. Brady and Alison saw. We buried you!" she yelled. This wasn't making any sense. She gripped his T-shirt and squeezed, and his hands covered hers as she tried to make sense of everything.

"Only Luke, Marcus, Ryan, Jack, and Harold knew," he said. "No one else could. I'm sorry. I didn't want to hurt you, and it damn near killed me, but it was the only way. It had to seem real. Everyone had to think I was dead. Luke said he would tell everyone after the funeral, after Mossad heard I was dead and no longer a threat to them. There was no other way."

His hands slid over her shoulders, and he leaned in and pressed a kiss to her forehead. His hands were on her face now, holding her, looking at her. Then he leaned in and pressed a kiss to her lips, a kiss she'd thought she'd never feel again. When he pulled back, he didn't let her go. She settled into his arms.

"But you were shot," she said. "I was told you were shot and killed. Brady said it had come through the window, and…"

He had said the man who held a gun at them had been killed, too, shot dead. It was a horrible situation. She looked up at Raymond and saw the grimness there.

"We didn't know if it would work. We had to plan something fast when we learned where Brady and Alison were being held. Harold is the best shot, according to Marcus. He was across the street with a long-range rifle, and I had on a bulletproof vest. I counted on Harold and put my trust in someone because my son said to. Luke had a blood bag, and he had me take ketamine before we got there. Apparently, his team supplied everything we needed without asking any questions. The drug is fast acting. It knocked me out and had me appearing dead. Harold shot and killed Saul shortly after. He was the man who was there that night with Ivan, the man you killed. They were never going to go away, because I was wanted for treason, and they weren't about to let me walk. Luke said the other three left with a photo of me dead on their phones. The funeral had to happen, because they had to believe it was real. I'm sorry, but it was the only way. I had to die. I'm so sorry for the pain I knew we had to bring you, and I hope you'll forgive me."

She wrapped her hands around his wrists, feeling him tuck her short dark hair behind her ears. "You look pretty damn good for a dead man," she said, then lifted her head, taking in the man she'd never thought she'd get her forever with.

He lowered his head again, pressed his forehead to hers and another kiss to her lips.

"You'll have to make it up to me," she breathed out after she pulled back.

"Since I'm now dead, I'll do more than that."

"So what does this mean for you and me?"

He ran his hands over her back and down, holding her against him. "It means we get a second chance at the lifetime we were cheated of."

"But Raymond O'Connell is dead."

"Yeah, but that's the thing about being dead: You get to come back as someone else."

As he pressed his hands to her cheeks again, she looked up into the face of the man she'd married so long ago, the father of her six children. Now here he was, with her again.

"And just so you know, Iris," he said, "we really are better together than apart."

Turn the page for a sneak peek of
THE RETURN OF THE O'CONNELLS the next book in *THE O'CONNELLS*
Available in print, eBook & audio

THE RETURN OF THE O'CONNELLS

Will life ever return to normal?

That's the question everyone in the O'Connell family has asked since their lives were turned upside down by a murder charge. With their father now back from the dead, the O'Connells are coming to grips with the idea that justice isn't equal. But despite the pending arrival of a new grandchild, and the fact that the family is settling into a new identity, trouble seems to always be one step away. This time, it could come from within, as a shadowy new enemy has found its way into the close-knit family and could ultimately destroy the bond the siblings share, forcing them to finally cut their losses and walk away from one another.

There was something about secrets: They had a way of making themselves felt long before anyone even learned of them. The O'Connells kept secrets, and they were good at that. It seemed they always had—from others, from each other. But secrets had a way of slipping out explosively, scandalously, and never without repercussions. That left the kinds of battle scars the average person couldn't see.

The O'Connells had two kinds of secrets. There was the kind they wanted to keep, but there was also the kind they wouldn't dare tell a soul, the kind that had to stay secret forever.

Now Karen had another secret of her own as she sat quietly in the passenger side of Jack's Mercedes, anything but the dutiful and obedient wife.

"You've said not two words since we left the office," Jack said.

There was something about the way he spoke to her, the edge, like an alpha. The way he watched her at times, she knew he wondered what she was keeping from him.

She took in the barren trees of another season settling upon them, the frigid dirty white packed at the sides of the freshly plowed roads, the exhaust from the vehicles ahead of them. She'd seen it all thousands of times before, except now it was as if she were seeing everything for the first time.

What was different?

Everything.

The phone call.

She pulled in a breath and glanced over to Jack, reminding herself that she needed to tell him, but again the words wouldn't come. "Have a lot on my mind," she replied.

He only nodded, but she could feel the weight of something being held back. Was it her, or was it him? She forced herself to glance back to Brady, who was staring out the side window. His dark hair needed a cut. He glanced back down to his phone, thumbing over the screen. There was something on his mind, too.

"Brady, you to haven't said much, either," Jack said, lifting his gaze to the rear-view mirror as he pulled up to the lights. "How was school today?"

"School's school," he replied. "What do you want me to say? I was given the option to take some elective courses to finish the school year with the other kids, because the only class I wanted is full, but I said hell no. I'm finishing the required math, and then I have enough credits and I'm out of there." He swiped his hands together. Could she blame him? "Is Luke coming back?"

Right. That was the other call she'd had.

Karen turned back to looking straight ahead, out the windshield, seeing the street she knew like the back of her hand, feeling the comfort of her husband's vehicle despite how different everything seemed.

"Yes, he called this morning."

"And what did he say, again? That he's bringing someone?" Jack said.

She needed to pull in another breath, feeling the tightness in her chest and the heaviness that settled inside her again.

"He said it was an accidental kiss with consequences, and he wants us to meet her, which is apparently his way of saying he met someone he really likes and is bringing her home with him to meet the family. This should be interesting."

"And he's going to be at Ryan's?" Brady said, a hopeful note in his voice.

She made herself look back at him, seeing something else in his expression. Right, Luke was his buddy, the brother he leaned on to keep his head straight, even though he was the one who was often gone at a moment's notice.

"No, Marcus's," she said, then realized maybe she'd forgotten to relay that text.

Jack shook his head.

"You forgot to mention that," he said, the edge in his voice slipping into that pissed-off tone he seemed to have been taking with her more and more as of late.

She made herself drag her gaze over to him, taking in the beard that had been growing in for three days now. He was settling into a look that was more messy bad boy than his usual classy style. She wondered if he had any idea. *Likely not.*

"Marcus lives just across the street from Ryan, so I'm at a loss to understand how that's a big deal," she said. "Besides, it was just a text. Do I need to report every single thing to you?" Even she didn't miss the sharpness in her voice, and for a moment she was positive Jack gripped the steering wheel that much harder.

"You two aren't going to start fighting again, are you?" Brady jumped in.

She had to remind herself he was the newest member of their family, her brother. Brady was perceptive, quiet, polite, and kept everything to himself, still finding his place among the O'Connells.

"We don't fight, Brady. Do we, Jack?" she said, and she didn't miss the rude sound Jack made in response as he pulled into Marcus's driveway and parked behind Charlotte's Subaru. The sheriff's car was parked out front, so she didn't need to wonder whether Marcus was still at work.

Jack took his time putting the car in park and turning off the engine, then gave everything to her with that one look. His icy blue eyes could hide things from her that she would've had no idea about. "We fight," he said. "You fight. Brady's right."

A smile tugged at Brady's lips as he climbed out of the car without saying a word and closed the back door, and she and Jack followed.

"Brady, it's called having a difference of opinion and standing your ground," she called out to Brady's back, as he was halfway to the house.

He didn't turn around as he kept walking, only lifted his hand and tossed out over his shoulder, "If that's what you want to call it, but I know fighting when I hear it—and I know not to ever take you on."

Then he was up the steps, and she found herself taking in Jack as she walked around the vehicle, pulling at her red coat, feeling the cold on her face, feeling the ice under her impractically high black boots.

"Careful," Jack said. "It seems Marcus needs to clear this snow better."

She didn't look over as she pressed her hand on the hood of the car, taking careful steps, but Jack walked around and offered his arm. He was almost the perfect gentleman, always there for her, though he never saw her point of view on anything.

"Marcus has a lot on his plate," she said. "And Brady really thinks we're fighting?"

Jack was walking carefully, holding on to her, until they reached the sidewalk, which had been cleared of snow. The cold bit her bare thighs over her impractical knee-high boots, and the early winter wind whipped under her dress.

"We do fight, Karen, or rather, you do."

There it was, her need to set him straight.

"Really?" she said. "Because how I see it is that you try to tell me what to do, and you never ask my opinion on anything before deciding, thinking you can just go and do whatever you want, whenever you want. Just know that I will never let you tell me what to do, and I'll never go along with something just because you can't be bothered to ask and check in with me. I honestly believe you expect me to just fall in line with your way of thinking…"

"So you disagree and argue just because, Karen? I often wonder if you'd ever just go along with something because I decided it was best or because you understand that I'm looking out for you. No! You make nothing easy." It came out quite sharply, and she could feel the passion in him.

The way he said it, Karen could feel something more coming.

"You mean I don't make it easy for you to steamroll me."

"No, I mean we're married," he said. "You're my wife,

Karen, even with everything this family has been through, all the secrets and lies. Maybe I just want a little peace for us, a little of you meeting me halfway, instead of feeling as if everything is a fight." He stopped at the bottom of the steps and faced her, pulling in a breath. When he let it out, she could see his frustration.

The inside door was still open, and they should've headed in, but Jack had something else on his mind. His expression had an edge, a hardness. He was distracted. She wondered what secret he was keeping. As she stared at the man she loved, she wondered whether this discontent would always exist between them.

"You know something, don't you?" she said, hearing the accusation in her voice. "You did something."

"My name's been tossed out to run for governor. I'm on the ticket."

There it was, the surprise she didn't want.

Jack glanced away a second and then back to her. "You knew it was coming, and so did I. I just didn't expect it now."

"That means…"

"I think you know what it means, Karen. We have to leave Livingston, and we'll have to close up shop on the law practice."

She just stared, feeling a heaviness settle right in her stomach, leaving her with that sick feeling that wouldn't go away.

"I see," she said,

and then she said nothing else, because this was just something she didn't want on her plate right now. She found herself turning to the steps to walk away, but his hand was on her, and he was right in her space, holding her so she couldn't leave.

"Don't do that," he said. "Don't just walk away. You think I don't get that you're pissed off and you don't want this? Neither do I, but you know about the favors I called in to fix things, to clean up after all those damn secrets your family had, to keep Marcus as sheriff and keep the vultures from our door. So is this how you're going to handle it? Because I'm not in the mood for you to dig your heels in and not give an inch."

She shook her head. "You're way off base, Jack. I don't care right now about the governor ticket, and I don't want to think about it or start asking you all the things I'm wondering, like why you couldn't bother telling me until now. Will there always be something that falls into that category where you think you don't need to tell me everything? Anyway, no, I'm not there yet, because I have stuff going on, too."

He was confused and unimpressed.

"What the hell are you talking about, Karen? What stuff—work or something personal, more secrets, something with your family?"

Oh, great, he was really going down that road again. He stepped back and was no longer touching her, but the early Montana winter cold was starting to sting a bit, and she supposed now was as good a time as any.

"No, no, and no," she said. "The doctor's office called me."

When a smile touched his lips, she forced herself to pull it together and continue.

"Don't get excited. They confirmed I was pregnant, but I lost the baby."

There it was. His expression filled with the same thing she hadn't been able to feel.

"Right," she said, then gestured with her thumb behind her. "I'm going in."

She started up the steps, and when she pulled open the door and glanced back to Jack, who was still standing there, staring out at nothing, she didn't have a clue what the hell he was thinking.

About the Author

"Lorhainne Eckhart is one of my go to authors when I want a guaranteed good book. So many twists and turns, but also so much love and such a strong sense of family."

(Lora W., Reviewer)

New York Times & USA Today bestseller Lorhainne Eckhart writes Raw Relatable Real Romance is best known for her big family romances series, where "Morals and family are running themes. Danger, romance, and a drive to do what is right will see you glued to the page." As one fan calls her, she is the "Queen of the family saga." (aherman) writing "the ups and downs of what goes on within a family but also with some suspense, angst and of course a bit of romance thrown in for good measure." Follow Lorhainne on Bookbub to receive alerts on New Releases and Sales and join her mailing list at LorhainneEckhart.com for her Monday Blog, books news, giveaways and FREE reads. With over 120 books, audiobooks, and multiple series published and available at all retailers now translated into six languages. She is a multiple recipient of the Readers' Favorite Award for Suspense and Romance, and lives in the Pacific Northwest on an island, is the mother of three, her oldest has autism and she is an advocate for never giving up on your dreams.

The O'Connells: The O'Connells of Livingston, Montana are not your typical family. A riveting collection of stories surrounding the ups and downs of what goes on within a family but also with some suspense, angst and of course a bit of romance thrown in for good measure "I thought I loved the Friessens, but I absolutely adore the O'Connell's. Each and every book has totally different genres of stories but the one thing in common is how she is able to wrap it around the family which is the heart of each story." (C. Logue)

The Friessens: An emotional big family romance series, the Friessen family siblings find their relationships tested, lay their hearts on the line, and discover lasting love! "Lorhainne Eckhart is one of my go to authors when I want a guaranteed good book. So many twists and turns, but also so much love and such a strong sense of family." (Lora W., Reviewer)

The Parker Sisters: The Parker Sisters are a close-knit family, and like any other family they have their ups and downs. "Eckhart has crafted another intense family drama…The character development is outstanding, and the emotional investment is high…" (Aherman, Reviewer)

The McCabe Brothers: Join the five McCabe siblings on their journeys to the dark and dangerous side of love! An intense, exhilarating collection of romantic thrillers you won't want to miss. — "Eckhart has a new series that is definitely worth the read. The queen of the family saga started this series with a spin-off of her wildly successful Friessen series." From a Readers' Favorite award—winning

author and "queen of the
family saga" (Aherman)

Lorhainne loves to hear from her readers! You can connect with me at:
www.LorhainneEckhart.com
lorhainneeckhart.le@gmail.com

The Outsider Series
The Forgotten Child (Brad and Emily)
A Baby and a Wedding *(An Outsider Series Short)*
Fallen Hero (Andy, Jed, and Diana)
The Search *(An Outsider Series Short)*
The Awakening (Andy and Laura)
Secrets (Jed and Diana)
Runaway (Andy and Laura)
Overdue *(An Outsider Series Short)*
The Unexpected Storm (Neil and Candy)
The Wedding (Neil and Candy)

The Friessens: A New Beginning
The Deadline (Andy and Laura)
The Price to Love (Neil and Candy)
A Different Kind of Love (Brad and Emily)
A Vow of Love, A Friessen Family Christmas

The Friessens
The Reunion
The Bloodline (Andy & Laura)
The Promise (Diana & Jed)
The Business Plan (Neil & Candy)
The Decision (Brad & Emily)
First Love (Katy)
Family First
Leave the Light On
In the Moment

In the Family
In the Silence
In the Charm
Unexpected Consequences
It Was Always You
The First Time I Saw You
Welcome to My Arms
Welcome to Boston
I'll Always Love You
Ground Rules
A Reason to Breathe
You Are My Everything
Anything For You
The Homecoming
Stay Away From My Daughter
The Bad Boy
A Place of Our Own
The Visitor
All About Devon
Long Past Dawn
How to Heal a Heart
Keep Me In Your Heart

The O'Connells
The Neighbor
The Third Call
The Secret Husband
The Quiet Day
The Commitment
The Missing Father
The Hometown Hero
Justice
The Family Secret

The Fallen O'Connell
The Return of the O'Connells
And The She Was Gone
The Stalker
The O'Connell Family Christmas
The Girl Next Door

The McCabe Brothers
Don't Stop Me (Vic)
Don't Catch Me (Chase)
Don't Run From Me (Aaron)
Don't Hide From Me (Luc)
Don't Leave Me (Claudia)
Out of Time

A Billy Jo McCabe Mystery
Nothing As it Seems
Hiding in Plain Sight
The Cold Case
The Trap
Above the Law

The Wilde Brothers
The One (Joe and Margaret)
The Honeymoon, A Wilde Brothers Short
Friendly Fire (Logan and Julia)
Not Quite Married, A Wilde Brothers Short
A Matter of Trust (Ben and Carrie)
The Reckoning, A Wilde Brothers Christmas
Traded (Jake)
Unforgiven (Samuel)
The Holiday Bride

Married in Montana
His Promise
Love's Promise
A Promise of Forever

The Parker Sisters
Thrill of the Chase
The Dating Game
Play Hard to Get
What We Can't Have
Go Your Own Way
A June Wedding

Kate & Walker
One Night
Edge of Night
Last Night

Walk the Right Road Series
The Choice
Lost and Found
Merkaba
Bounty
Blown Away: The Final Chapter

The Saved Series
Saved
Vanished
Captured

Single Titles
He Came Back
Loving Christine